Pl
Yo
or

CUSTO

MAKING STUFF UP

*Bill James titles available from
Severn House Large Print*

Tip Top
Hear Me Talking to You
Between Lives
Double Jeopardy

MAKING STUFF UP

Bill James

Severn House Large Print
London & New York

This first large print edition published 2009
in Great Britain and the USA by
SEVERN HOUSE PUBLISHERS of
9-15 High Street, Sutton, Surrey, SM1 1DF.
First world regular print edition published 2006 by
Severn House Publishers, London and New York.

British Library Cataloguing in Publication Data

James, Bill, 1929-
 Making stuff up. - Large print ed.
 1. Universities and colleges - Finance - Fiction 2. College
 teachers - Fiction 3. Large type books
 I. Title
 823.9'14[F]

ISBN-13: 978-0-7278-7749-9

Printed and bound in Great Britain by
MPG Books Ltd, Bodmin, Cornwall.

One

Naturally, when the Minister and his retinue arrived, Caspar Ballaugh himself showed them around the campus, as it could be quite reasonably called. Ballaugh had met the Minister a few times before and judged him less obviously in the wrong job than many of his recent predecessors. Some would argue this said next to nothing. Ballaugh regarded that as sweeping, though. Just the same, he did recognize that Governments – and especially the present Government – seemed to avoid appointing politicians with over-obvious intellect to the Education posts. Ballaugh thought he saw why. There was a sort of kindness to it, a sort of fine wisdom. The brightest Westminster people had probably enjoyed a smart and effective education and therefore knew how the system ideally should be. But they would soon discover how glaringly it now wasn't.

This could lead to despair, then listlessness, then paralysis. Clearly, painful – and bad for the country. Governments aimed to seem hot on progress in Education. Surely everyone recalled that famous statement of political priorities: 'Education, education, education.' Ballaugh wondered whether this nicely timed repetition contained a promise by the Government that its school and college policies would ensure every grown-up could count to three.

New in his post, the Minister had let it be known as a taster for this visit that he 'personally' intended to call in on every university during the next six months. He'd addressed all Principals and Vice-Chancellors via a general email saying he meant to 'survey and celebrate *on the ground* the achievements and, above all, deep potential, of a higher education system justly admired worldwide'.

The Minister hated being called Minister. 'You might fucking well want me to baptize you, Caspar,' he'd said. 'You see a dog collar?' The Minister loved humour and intelligent swearing. In some aspects, he sought ordinariness, a kind of special, officed, chauffeured ordinariness. He was a devoted pleb, but pleb with a gorgeous salary and dreamscape allowances. He had told

Ballaugh he believed in basics and that basics were his unvarying career guide and his revered touchstone. Such rich, academic terms as 'research criteria' and 'discipline parameters' evidently made him queasy. He loathed talk to turn what he called 'heavy', considered it inappropriate.

When he grew bored, the Minister tended to come out with poor, ancient jokes, often about people he regarded as stuffy and adrift from basics. Although Ballaugh certainly did not object to hearing All Souls – the very élite, Oxford, postgraduate college – referred to as Arseholes college, this seemed short of novelty because Ballaugh had first made the wordplay years ago. He did chuckle along with the Minister, out of politeness and fellow-feeling. Incidentally, even now, it always enraged Caspar – maybe more than it would enrage the Minister – to read in someone's biography that he had been 'admitted to a Fellowship at All Souls by examination'. The capital F strutted and boomed, didn't it? And that word 'admitted', backed up with 'by examination', was so damn pat and pushy. Ballaugh invariably took this form of boasting as a roundabout and dirty attack on himself and his academic background, possibly suggesting that, if *he* had tried the All Souls examination, no way would he have been admitted to an upper case Fellowship. Or if he tried it now, come to that. Well, Fuck Off, upper case.

The Minister's first name was Maurice but he preferred Mo, mainly as an escape from any comparison with what he called 'simpering Maurice Chevalier', and then for not being gender specific, because women named Maureen or Maud often downdressed that to Mo these days. Mo's father held Government office under Wilson or Callaghan in the seventies, poor sod, so the family could be relied on for bags of half-baked, soft-focus political energy and attitude, plus plenty of shagged-out, worthy wordage. Ballaugh had actually heard Mo use the phrases 'cutting edge' and 'hands-on' without the slightest stumble. Ballaugh thought it would be difficult to loathe Mo absolutely, though, at least to date. He had a ramshackle, off-and-on winsomeness to him which mysteriously seemed increased rather than cancelled by the hugeness of his head. Winsomeness from someone with a head that large somehow carried the happy bonus of surprise. Mo would be around forty-six, forty-seven, thin – making his head appear even bigger, like a sunflower – his eyes darkish but bright and seeming to signal serene and adjustable faithfulness to a cause. Clearly, this could be a fucking pain, but he probably wouldn't be allowed to get far with it at his middling rank.

Ahead of this visit, Ballaugh had ordered in two copies for the library of Mo's father's autobiography published a couple of years ago. Many said that if those old time Labour papers, the *Daily Herald* and *Reynolds News,* still existed, they would certainly have published quite long extracts. Ballaugh made sure the books' newness was given some educated trampling with Hush Puppy-type, unhobnailed boots, to suggest keen but considerate use; and, of course, he fixed for a crowded string of back-dated borrowing entries, some stamped, some handwritten, as if renewed by telephone because the borrower was too enthralled by it in his room to break off from reading and go to the library. Ballaugh looked at the index and found the book, called *For The People,* contained two mentions of Mo – though as Maurice, naturally – both pretty favourable, given what Mo was like, and supposing his father knew at the time of writing. On the campus look-around, Ballaugh did get Mo into the Politics section of the library where *For The People* had been placed at Minister eye level, after some jigging of alphabetical-by-author sequence on the shelves. 'Ah,' he said. 'Father's vision statement.'

'Well, this *is* unusual,' Ballaugh replied.

'What?'

'For there to be copies in. We have more, of course, the others on loan. But I gather they're generally *all* out. Range.'

'What?'

'Range,' Ballaugh replied. 'That's the word. *For The People* has real *range* to it. Dimensions. Scale. Students like books that give them the true *feel* and *impulse* of an era, yet while also scrupulous about significant detail. I'm only an Economics and Business graduate, but can still appreciate the ... well, the historical *range* of this volume,' Ballaugh explained. 'Yes, "range" has to be the term. Would that all politicians were justified in summing up their life as *for* the people, Mo!'

'It's easy to *say* one is for the people, but dad genuinely cared about them.'

'I've never heard it denied,' Ballaugh replied. Maybe the present Prime Minister's autobiography could be called not quite *For The People* but *Fool The People,* possibly questioning Abraham Lincoln's pious dictum that you couldn't fool all the people all the time.

Mo said: 'Dad always knew that the people – I mean, the people as *people* – this is the essential, Caspar, the people *as* people – you see, he always knew they were out there. Sometimes, during my childhood, dad would gaze from the lounge window and tell me, "Maurice, the people are out there, the people as *people*. Never forget it, my boy. They are an abiding, influential factor and relevant to all politics."'

'Simple perception, yet unquestionably perception.'

'Yes, I think I can reasonably state that this instinct has happily been passed down to one's self, Casp. Perhaps he knew that must happen. I don't boast of it. How could I? Simply in the genes. Or like an inheritance, but not an inheritance cut by the Chancellor's death duties!' This joke seemed to make him think of property. 'You get a sort of manor house as tied cottage with your job, don't you? Architecturally interesting I gather. Can we have a look while my folk nose around a bit more here?'

Ballaugh rang Fiona to say they were coming. She had never met Mo but Ballaugh knew she'd give a grand welcome up to a point. Fiona felt a real, convulsive pity for most politicians. She used to say that if either of the children, Piers or Gabriel, turned that way, she'd kill herself, after first killing whichever child it was, or both if the two did it. Ballaugh regarded her standpoint as noble yet naive and overstated. 'The world has to be run, Fiona,' he'd said once. 'Who else but politicians suit?'

'Oh, I know, I know, the poor put-upon dears,' she replied. 'They deserve all those paperclip expenses on top of their pay and the terrific holidays – more even than yours.'

The house went back to Georgian times and had fine chimneys and windows. Ballaugh was not really into architecture, but realized it mattered to many people, possibly even Mo. For almost two centuries the house belonged to the Hith-Entrive family, one of those dynasties who'd established themselves as landowners and farmers, then moved successfully to industrial manufacture and export during the late nineteenth century. Ballaugh knew they'd started as Hith only. Perhaps that had come to seem thin and vulnerable to the family. The hyphen and the Entrive bit appeared to have been added thanks to an important marriage around 1820. This came soon after that bloody Peterloo riot at Manchester, which convinced the upper classes they'd better bind together in case of revolution and head rolling copied from France. Apparently the major Victorian poet, Matthew Arnold, knew the contemporary Hith-Entrives and stayed here with them two or three times around 1850 while travelling as a schools' inspector. Probably this association had appealed to the university when buying Vallin Court as official residence for its Vice-Chancellors in 1995, the last of the local Hith-Entrives having moved for a better climate to Spain. This kind of university could benefit from any links with past distinguished figures. It hadn't had time to produce its own yet. Ballaugh himself liked the association.

Pleasant oil and watercolour pictures and sketches of the house, gardens and surrounding fields as they used to be hung in the large hall. Some showed members of a fox hunt assembling. Mo said: 'We have changed all that.' Another picture featured a shepherd and his flock near animal pens which looked to Ballaugh as if skilfully made from plaited branches and boughs. Someone from the English department who'd been up to Ballaugh's house for dinner thought the pens as shown might have given Matthew Arnold the notion for a famous line, 'Go, Shepherd, and untie the wattled cotes', which figured in one of his poems, *The Scholar-Gypsy* apparently. Ballaugh had installed a special wall light above this picture to give it projection. He liked to be 'in tune', as it were, with old manual crafts. Although modern business and its precisions and mysteries fascinated him still, he recognized and respected those elementary but worthwhile ways of the past. As Vice-Chancellor he made a point now and then of telling the university's History staff they must not by any means think of themselves or their subject as in decay. He often read some history.

Ballaugh explained about the wattled cotes to Mo, '"wattled" meaning woven and "cotes" the actual enclosures, you see.'

'We think you've handled staff cuts very well, Casp,' Mo replied.

Which 'we' was that? Right up to Cabinet mention? Or just Mo and his Civil Servants? Ballaugh said: 'There were clear guidelines.'

'Well, I hope so. We see as a priority the need to expand departments likely to attract overseas students, and therefore funding from their countries of origin. And then comes the unfortunate parallel budgetary requirement to trim areas *not* likely to be of interest to those countries. The rationalization you've managed in that rather fancy outfit, for instance – so right.'

'There are several.'

'But the really far out one,' Mo said.

'Creative Writing?'

14

'Something like that. What is it?'

'What?'

'Creative Writing.'

'They write.'

'What?'

'Stories, poems.'

'Like Eng. Lit., you mean?' Mo asked. 'I'm definitely not against Eng. Lit. This is a contributing heritage.'

'No, they do their own stories and poems. Even plays. From scratch, absolutely.'

'You mean making stuff up?' Mo said.

'Right.'

'This is not like looking at, say, Shakespeare and Thomas Hardy, but just putting down things on paper they've thought up for themselves?'

'That's it. Very big in America.'

'What?'

'Creative Writing. It's moving in here.'

'Mind you, Casp, I don't say there isn't a place for that kind of thing – the creative. I've never minded a good poem. And novels. *The Ragged Trousered Philanthropist.* Dad adored that one. Education has to take in all sorts or where are we, Casp? Have you heard the phrase "Renaissance man?" Well, yes, I'm sure you have. Or woman, obviously, these days. Meaning interested in all sorts. Fullness. This can be a plus. But there are boundaries. Obviously, foreign students are not going to be keen to learn about writing poems or what have you in English. If they want to compose along those lines they'll do it at home and in their own languages. You were sharp to spot that, Casp. Engineering. Business. Medicine. These are the subjects that draw our visitors. Sharp, sharp, Casp.'

'Here's Fiona now,' Ballaugh said. He introduced them. She stood with Mo, gazing in a deep sort of way at the sheep scene. Ballaugh saw that if this was what Mo wanted to do, Fiona wanted him to do it. She thought of politicians as almost eternally badgered into phoniness and nerves by their leaders, their constituents, the media and the future's hoped-for approval. Fiona would feel that for Mo to reach this spell of apparent self-lessness and calm through gazing at art amounted to a therapy or laxative, bringing the pressures on him down, and clearing his body, for a time at least, of the political game's mad, poisonous, crucial egomania. Fiona never voted. She regarded support for any candidate as a kind of irresponsible victimization, like allowing a child burger-type food, with no regard for later obesity and unsightliness. Electoral success should not be encouraged. Oh, it gave the candidate an initial thrill, she didn't deny that – jolly, megaphoned thanks around the streets from an open-decked bus – but then it committed him/her to possibly decades of fatuous, craven awfulness, and almost certainly several years. This had to be cruel. She would mention a string of MPs and ministers in whom she saw the terrible effects.

There had been previous visits by politicians to Vallin Court – the city's three MPs at various times on business, two Shadow Education Ministers for briefing, and two French Deputies researching the British university system. Fiona pampered all of them, as Caspar had once seen her pamper a cat unfatally hit by a Vauxhall. Inevitably, her kindliness was sometimes read as sexual come-on. Mo might wonder now. She stood very close to him in the hall and Ballaugh saw one of his long legs twitch marginally, probably not on account of wattled cotes. Fiona had been at the scent bucket – 'Tantalize', or something else unmild. Last year, one of the local MPs became really frisked up by the warmth and attention she gave him. Ballaugh understood how it could happen. After all, few politicians would actually *expect* to be pitied, and assumed any attention given them arose instead from esteem or possible awe. They might be *for* the people, but they expected a reverence *from* the people as thanks for being for them. *They* thought they'd pulled off something worthwhile and enviable by getting into Westminster or even local councils. And, no matter what turds they looked, some of the males really believed they radiated Kennedy-type magic – or was it Kissinger? – 'the aphrodisiac of power?' Ballaugh suspected that what many of them had *for* the people was kept in their trousers, or not. On the whole, he believed nothing developed between Fiona and the MP, though her wish to comfort could be powerful. It might be especially powerful towards Mo who was not just an MP but a Minister, poor fuck, and so, for Fiona, in extra need of kindness and recuperation. Possibly she wouldn't feel watercolours could work that on their own and wonder if she should offer Mo more.

'I don't object to this kind of house,' he said.

'I'm glad,' Fiona replied.

'Not at all,' Mo said.

'Which kind?' Fiona asked.

'It has, or had, class implications, clearly,' Mo said. 'Fox-hunting. Ground-down shepherds having to wattle their own cotes. For decades, centuries, capitalism flagrantly hung out here.'

'I suppose you have to worry about that, you poor dear,' Fiona said. 'Is it referred to as "image", I wonder?'

'This property gave the squirearchical touch, or even above,' Mo said.

'Above,' Ballaugh replied. 'Prime gentry.'

'And so in the twenty-first century we install you, Fiona, and you, Casp! That's our rejoinder!'

Ballaugh still had trouble with 'we' and 'our' in Mo's thinking. Whose rejoinder? The Government's? The people's? Mo's and his staff's?

'If the house is an embarrassment, I suppose we could live in something smaller,' Fiona replied.

They entered the wide, panelled, high-ceilinged drawing room. Ballaugh handed around drinks and Mo examined the windows and the lawns they looked on to, then pondered an enormous, original fireplace. 'I like the, well, message in it,' he said. 'Not just the fireplace. All of it. The house. The style. The setting.'

Ballaugh said: 'Well, yes, we—'

'When I say I like the message, I mean, obviously, the message contained in the changes we have imposed,' Mo replied. Now, he seemed to spot the uncertainties in 'we' and added: 'When I say "we" I suppose I mean to some extent time – but it is time with our assistance.' Our? But he didn't explain that. 'If I consider this house as it was and as it is today I think one word. This is a word that sums it all up.'

' "Refurbishment?" ' Fiona asked.

'That word is "Outreach,"' Mo declared. In expression he gave it glamour and holiness.

'This is certainly a word I've heard,' Fiona said.

'I expect so! Oh, I expect so indeed!' Mo cried. 'Yes, I expect you *have* heard of it.' He chuckled a while at what he apparently took to be Fiona's witty understatement.

'Oh, yes, meaning, I think,' Fiona said, 'that universities should no longer be sealed-off communities of scholars and intellectuals but must engage with that wider community, the community to which we all belong, whether or not we are scholars and intellectuals. You can't go wrong with the word "community" these days, can you?'

Ballaugh realized she must have been mugging up some of the jargon and felt touched by her effort. Off and on she could be very dutiful.

'*Proactively* engage with,' Mo said. 'Reach out to the general community. Hence that rallying term, "Outreach".'

'Caspar speaks of this now and then,' Fiona said.

'I expect so,' Mo replied, plus another chuckle. 'Oh, yes, I expect so. After all, it's only the essence of our Education philosophy!'

'Clearly important,' Fiona said.

'The concept of Outreach puts such a house as this in its place, you see,' Mo said. 'Gives the house its identity. Its new, current, transformed identity. When I say "putting the house in its place" I'm referring, of course, to changing it from the blatant privilege it once had – its very core then. It trumpeted status, selfish wealth, social rank. No more. Now, instead, we have ... well, what do we have? We have status, yes, but another kind of status – benign, community-based, brilliantly democratic. We have you, Fiona, and Caspar as occupants. And what, dear Fiona, do you and Caspar symbolize?'

'This is fascinating, Mo,' she replied.

'Outreach,' Mo said. 'Caspar, as head of this university, *is* Outreach. And you, Fiona, are obviously part of it. Displacing what Casp calls "prime gentry" as residents we have Vice-Chancellor Caspar Ballaugh, and what Vice-Chancellor Caspar Ballaugh *signifies*. The so-called prime gentry built their manor house and surrounded it with big grounds so as deliberately to set a difference and a distance between themselves and the people. But now, you see, to use a phrase made familiar by Dad, we are *for* the people. The difference and distance exist no longer. Outreach is *for* the people and Casp and the university *are* Outreach – and Casp is here, in the property. And you, also, of course, Fiona.'

'Well, yes,' Fiona said.

'Or take myself,' Mo said.

'You must really have thought things out, Mo,' Fiona said.

'In previous times, if someone visiting this then distinguished house were called Maurice he would not allow this to be shortened to Mo,' Mo replied. 'Oh, dear no. Hardly in tone then with the property and its pretensions. I say *then*. But we have brought our progress, haven't we? There is consequently a grand normality about me – as Mo, I mean.'

'Well, yes,' Fiona replied.

'This has often been remarked on,' Ballaugh said.

'A cheek-by-jowlness – cheek-by-jowl with those people whom we are so emphatically *for* – I mean the people as *people*.'

'Mo is very focused on people as *people*, Fiona,' Ballaugh said. That vast concept-stuffed cranium might put the wind up people as *people* if Mo grew too cheek-by-jowly with them. And Ballaugh would not want him getting cheek-by-jowly with Fiona. Did she rate as one of the people as *people*?

'Politicians have to be philosophers as well as all their other chores,' Fiona said.

Mo glowed with fantasy, but constructive fantasy. 'You know, I like to think of the spirits of folk who once lived here returning – I mean returning, resurrected from history – and, possibly despite themselves, obliged to acclaim the social transformation embodied in Vallin Court's new occupants, Fiona and Casp,' Mo replied. 'It might be that I'll request the university authorities to consider a change from that now not very appropriate name, "Vallin Court". It reeks of exclusivity. You'll ask, Change it to what? But could we do better than "Outreach"? Could we?'

'Always inventiveness, perception, initiative,' Fiona said. 'Will you never rest, Mo?'

'When my office were preparing the itinerary for this tour I insisted they put Caspar first,' Mo replied. 'But why first, I hear you ask? Why? Because, of course, he is our supreme Outreach leader, an Outreach pathfinder, a standard bearer, pioneeringly proactive for Outreach. I want to be able to pass on what I learn here to the places I'll see subsequently.'

'Will you be able to get Oxford and Cambridge to do Outreach?' Fiona asked. 'Aren't they inclined to be a bit snooty? Is it Cambridge that goes on about "intellectual rigour"? Does that square with a come-one-come-all invitation to the general community?'

'Well, we certainly do some Outreach here,' Ballaugh said.

'Oh, some!' Mo cried. 'Modesty!'

'We're expanding it gradually,' Ballaugh said.

'Oh, gradually!' Mo cried. 'You're a front-runner in Outreach, Casp. An exemplar.' His voice fell and he grew confiding, secretive. 'Casp, I'm here now to say there's reliable rumour about a gong for your Outreach activity. That's the real reason I wanted to come out to your home and meet Fiona. Although architecture and watercolours definitely have their attraction, and I would never regard them as negligible, my purpose is other. This award buzz involves both of you. From that, you can deduce we're talking an outright peerage, Casp. And, so, a Ladyship. Deserved. Utterly deserved. We need a voice like yours in the Lords, Casp. Other university heads have collected peer-

Kent Libraries,
Registration and Archives
www.kent.gov.uk/libraries
Tel: 03000 41 31 31

Items that you have borrowed

Title: Another country [text(large print)]
ID: C155365695
Due: 28 August 2021

Title: Making stuff up [text(large print)]
ID: C153540773
Due: 28 August 2021

Title: So much pretty [text(large print)]
ID: C155346011
Due: 28 August 2021

Total items: 3
Account balance: £0.00
07/08/2021 11:48
Borrowed: 3
Overdue: 0
Reservation requests: 0
Ready for collection: 0

Thank you for using self service

ages. That lad at Lampeter. You will achieve what on the face of it might seem impossible: you will bring more and more people into meaningful, productive contact with the university while also improving its league rating. I know you'll take this institution towards the select list of most distinguished universities, the so-called Russell Group, Casp. You can do it. You are well on the way to doing it. Oxford and Cambridge are there, naturally, but so are Nottingham, Bristol, Cardiff. You will disprove that dismal forecast about university education, "more means worse". If Vice-Chancellors elsewhere bleat to me about their difficulties with implementing Outreach, or even question its basic worth, I speak your name, Casp. I tell them that Casp Ballaugh can develop Outreach with one hand, while intelligently culling staff in some departments irrelevant to the foreign recruiting programme with the other. Of course, you get some abuse, Casp, on the Internet, through the media. You'll handle that, crush that.'

'And *you*, Mo – what about a gong for you?' Fiona said. 'Working like this, travelling everywhere, poor duck, listening all the time for buzzes, interpreting them, deciding which buzzes are only buzzes and which substantive. You should have recognition, reward, surely.'

'Not appropriate,' Mo replied. 'One has one's duties to the people. One works, one strives, *for* the people. To follow these compulsions is enough – is why I and others in politics exist.'

Two

A couple of days after Mo's visit Ballaugh
had heard no more from him, and therefore
assumed that, in general, the verdict remained favourable. This was despite redundancy
troubles in some departments, and Vallin
Court's flagrantly capitalist history, though
now triumphantly corrected on behalf of the
people whom Mo believed in being definitely for.

Leaving his office, Ballaugh set out towards the Students' Union building where
editors of the university magazine, *College
Collage*, had laid on a university-funded
buffet lunch to mark its ten years of exis-
tence. Copies of a special celebratory issue
would be available. As Ballaugh understood
things, invitations had gone out to all sorts.
He needed to be there. Influential people
kept an eye on student literature and journalism these days, hoping to spot a young
star and sign her/him up, especially a *her* and
with nice eyes, hair and skin, for the dust-

cover picture. Ballaugh might have a chance to talk to newspaper editors, public relations executives, broadcasting company chiefs, publishers. Obviously, folk like that could be a real help with his large scheme for the university's advancement. As an instance, it would be a magnificent plus if a contributor to *College Collage,* or more than one, were chosen by some of these concerns for early, distinguished exposure in their fields. He'd read about students at other places – mostly Oxford and Cambridge, of course, oh, *so* fucking of course – who began to make a mark in the media game long before they'd graduated.

Despite Mo's praise and the hint of a peerage, Ballaugh suffered big and confusing anxieties about his post here. Lately, he had been reading, rereading, Kingsley Amis's university novel of the 1950s, *Lucky Jim,* and a phrase there reached out – out reached, you might say – and took a real windpipe grip on him. It was 'even at a place like this'. The words came in one of lecturer Jim Dixon's hate storms about Welch, his boss, Dixon being the book's hero, or *anti*-hero. How had Welch become Professor of History *'even at a place like this?'* Jim asked himself in the Amis story (Ballaugh's unhappy italics.)

Ballaugh wondered sometimes whether *he*

presided over such a place, a place like that. Regardless of what Mo said, this university was not really much to write home about, was it, except possibly by the students? *Did* they write home about it? Email home about it, and in satisfactorily mounting numbers to foreign homes, supplying foreign money? What did they say? Oh, hell. It had, of course, also been Kingsley Amis who first used that depressing mot quoted by Mo – God, 'mot by Mo', a chime! – on increased student admissions: 'more means worse'. Today, might he have extended the phrase to 'more means worse, especially from over-seas'? Amis did not care all that much for abroad. He liked it here.

Amis knew universities. He'd been an undergraduate and graduate in one and taught at a couple of others. He was remembered, too, for amending a report that spoke of the need to extend higher education and take up 'untapped talent'. He'd revised it to 'tapped untalent'. Did this university already tap untalent? Did Outreach aim to tap even more of it? Under the current dispensation, did a university become better by recruiting worse students, as long as the foreign ones came bearing boodle? And yet, weren't the alternatives to Outreach places like All Souls, Oxford, with their odious exclusiveness, glaring top-doggery and privileged wine cellars: the damn upper case F Fellowships awarded 'by examination'; by disgustingly competitive and flagrantly élitist examination, deliberately and proactively fashioned not *for* the people at all but to keep the fucking people *out*, or all but the minutest, approved fraction of them? He abominated that fluting high-table tradition at Oxford and Cambridge – lecturers being so witty and polymath over their dinner and good-year claret.

As to Oxford and Cambridge, Ballaugh hated quadrangles. But, in pathetic imitation of an Oxbridge college, there was a quadrangle of sorts just outside his office, which he had to pass through now on his way to the Union. He loathed what he thought of as the poncy isolationism of quadrangles, with their bit of trampled, struggling grass and damn wood benches, as if for great minds to sit and think about juicy themes, and talk about juicy themes, while nicely cut off from all the noisy, workaday stuff beyond. There were times when he wanted to stand at the centre of it, take out his cock and piss in the grandest arc he could manage, taking in at least two of the benches, occupied or not. The benches had small commemorative metal plaques on them, to commemorate previous commemorable figures in the university's pathetically short life, including Ballaugh's immediate, very commemorable predecessor, Andreas Main, and a couple of former Bursars who'd unarguably kept their noses virtually clean, so could be commemorated also. God, the sad, frantic hunt for tradition. One day, he'd get a bench himself most probably. It was that sort of place, unless he could change it. Mind, some girl student arses he would not mind sitting on him while their owners pondered his plaque.

As he strolled, Ballaugh could dwell on all kinds of tensions and contradictions. They brought him private agonies. The Government's Higher Education Statistics Agency recently published some very chewy league tables. One of these listed universities in order of merit according to the number of undergraduates, foreign and Brit., who actually completed their course and successfully took a degree, a reasonable requirement. Cambridge came out supreme at 97.3% with Oxford second (95.9) and the London School of Economics third (94.8). Durham, Nottingham, Bristol, Exeter and Warwick also did well.

But, alongside such figures, appeared another clutch. These catalogued the universities which, in the Government's view, were criminally deficient at opening their doors to a wide intake of students, and, instead, seemed tilted towards independent schools. Oxford headed these culprits, with 44.6% from independents. Cambridge followed (42.4). LSE, Durham, Nottingham, Bristol, Exeter and Warwick all featured in the top twenty. This seemed to indicate that the universities which excelled at getting students to finish the course they'd chosen – yes, probably a decent enough aim for a university, after all – were not much cop at making themselves generally available; and, in fact, some might face Government financial penalties for their stubborn choosiness. Did this mean that to be good a university had to be bad; to succeed it had to fail?

Obviously, Ballaugh understood the complexities. Sticking around until the end of their three-year stint might be easier for private school pupils. They'd probably have family money behind them, and so the fees laid on all students by Government would be less burdensome than for many state school pupils. Just the same, Ballaugh found the statistics tough to reconcile. His place here did not figure in the exclusive group, of course; and it came so near the bottom of the tally for successful graduations it was almost missing from there, too. He would not get punished, but neither would he be able to go on attracting many students if the drop-out rate didn't improve. Or he'd attract only students who couldn't get in anywhere else, were dismally below standard, and therefore not competent to survive the course. This would push his drop-out rate even higher, meaning yet fewer students of any quality opted to come here, and meaning, also, that the dependence on foreign fees grew. And so on. God! They'd make him a Lord for this?

Mo apparently considered Outreach one of the true means to improve the university's rating, and he knew how to voice his views whenever asked for them, and probably when not asked also. But Mo was a politician, and, for fuck's sake, the son of a politician! This busy legislator had been brought up on unmatchable junk slogans and the sweetest, sanctimonious gibberish as other kids were brought up on Lego and Sugar Puffs. Ballaugh certainly had moments of sympathy for Outreach, and, under modish – Mo-dish – orders, did try to apply bits of it. Yes, perhaps a university ought to aim for universality.

But Ballaugh thought he saw, also, another way to get this place ahead. And to get it ahead was what he'd been appointed for, what all Vice-Chancellors were appointed for, obviously. Even Mo wanted him to make it to the Russell Group, despite being for the people. And many of those people would be watching, looking at the multitudinous league tables in the *Daily Telegraph,* tables not just to do with inclusiveness-exclusiveness and degree completions, but the number of First Class Honours and the quality of post-graduate research. Yes, among his other drool, Mo had spelled out that Ballaugh's purpose must be to get this institution into that top-notch, Russell clique of universities, including, of course, Oxbridge, but some fortunate provincial spots, too. As a possible means to crash this smug consistory – naturally, most of them appeared in the censured and despised over-exclusive, disgustingly selective list – Ballaugh decided something more than a decent shot at Outreach might be needed. He had spotted an additional, possibly very useful factor.

Lately, loud hints had surfaced that the local metropolitan council fancied competing for the title European City of Culture, an award made every four years. Ballaugh was advised by some people of judgement that this need not necessarily be a farcically hopeless bid. Hadn't Liverpool won its bid for 2008? The ECOC Committee tended to avoid obvious candidates such as Florence, or Paris or Salzburg, and liked to surprise with kindly, encouraging, off-beat choices. As Ballaugh calculated, if the city won this honour, and he and colleagues had notably involved themselves in the campaign, the university could pick up a share of the considerable renown and prestige. This might be a more direct method to secure an improved rating than Outreach, honourable as the concept of Outreach almost definitely might be. Some doubted it – Roffe, head of Creative Writing, for instance. However, there would be good financial implications. Under recent legislation, the best universities could charge students extra tuition fees – top-up fees, so called – in order to maintain their status as the best. Ballaugh aimed to reach that category, Outreach included, but not *entirely* through Outreach. The desperate need for foreign infusions might then be lessened. One major trouble with money from abroad was that it could be very variable and subject to changes – subject to stoppage, in fact – when regimes changed. Ballaugh had become accustomed to watching the International News pages in the heavy Press for news of coups.

As he saw it, any university, *even a place like this* as now, *must* be notably involved in all major cultural efforts made by its host city. That, surely, was what Outreach meant, even though, yes, a competition in Culture unavoidably appeared ... well, competitive, discriminatory, élitist. Confusing. But these days, universities plainly could not stand apart and shut off. Town versus gown had become an antique and stupid rivalry. A university reached out to its neighbourhood and offered benefits – the whole worthy life-long learning bag and general access. All right, this could mean tapping untalent, but such risks might be worth a bit of a go, and were in any case impeccably fashionable thanks to Mo and those around Mo in Westminster. Reciprocating, the neighbourhood must likewise reach out, embracing and revering the university as one of its prized institutions, *even a place like this* – though a place Ballaugh felt convinced he could transform, given some luck. But was there luck on offer?

Although he abhorred the quadrangle, and all the pretentious, scholarly, quibbling quadrangular thinking that went with it, a couple of hours later, on his way back from the *College Collage* party, Ballaugh sat himself down on the Andreas Main bench. Never had he used any of the furniture before,

36

other than as targets in his wet arcing fantasy. But, now, after that terrible, flaring incident at the party, he was upset and disorientated. He'd like a spell of solitude and recovery before he returned to his office. *So* terrible and flaring, the incident, and full of grim significance for the university, and him.

The party had, in fact, been a very reasonable and promising occasion until Lucy Corth's sudden, inflamed, unhinged, symbolic intrusion, screaming at him about her terminated contract as a Creative Writing tutor – the most flagrant display yet of the rancorous resentment at Ballaugh's unavoidable trimming programme in those departments poor at drawing foreign students – Religious Studies, Classics, Fine Arts and, yes, Creative Writing. Had he ever heard a woman call a man a cunt before in a public gathering, particularly while standing on a plastic, stackable chair for attention? Post feminism he thought women no longer regarded the word 'cunt' as abuse and would not wish to confer it on a male, especially a loathed male. But unquestionably 'cunt' as used by Corth was not a compliment or even mere background. Had he deserved that?

He did some breathing exercises now and, to disguise his state from students passing through the quadrangle, opened the anniversary edition of *College Collage* he'd been given. It looked professional. On the Contents page under Fiction, he saw the name of Dr Leonard Maldave, another Creative Writing tutor – but not fired, yet. As part of his procedure for quietening himself after the Corth episode, Ballaugh turned to this contribution. In fact, Len Maldave represented the university on the city council's European City of Culture Committee, concerned with early preparatory work for the award bid. Ballaugh had never been sure Maldave was right for this responsibility, but Basil Roffe, C. W.'s professor, declined to attend. Maldave lacked what Ballaugh would regard as oomph. But he had let the membership stand, largely because people argued that Maldave, as a published novelist, carried status. A Maldave colleague in Creative Writing – another not yet flung out – had told Ballaugh in the usual polite, excoriating hate terms these people applied to one another: 'Len's by no means negligible, in my view and that of at least one other. Two novels out. These could not entirely fairly be described as negligible, either. I'm pretty certain I saw the words "sagely mild and untrendy" in a review of *Nursery Scimitar*.'

Ballaugh had tried *Nursery Scimitar* and the other one, the *Sandwich Board*, or was it

Placard, and thought they certainly showed stiff-covered quality – but memorable quality? *Nursery Scimitar* did not mean an actual scimitar in a nursery, more a metaphorical or symbolic usage – even emblematic – which Ballaugh thought he had sorted during his reading of the book. He could see that the title might grab through its suggestion of horror. Less winningly, in Ballaugh's opinion, both novels did a lot of very lumpy meditating around the edge of their tales about the actual *nature* of novels and of fiction altogether – the problem of whether fiction had its own, as it were, truth, or Truth, and whether this 'truth' or 'Truth' might in some ways be more true than the supposed truths of so-called factual works. Ballaugh, trained in Economics and Business Studies, could see this must be an interesting topic to novelists, but might not be an Outreach topic, not, say, a pub bar topic. People at the boozer for big screen cricket were not going to spend any time arguing whether *Nursery Scimitar* got things more fucking right than *Wisden*.

Admittedly, Maldave's tales had reached out in at least some degree to Ballaugh, who was not a novelist, and who had been educated from books containing facts proven by observation and experiences. But as Vice-

Chancellor and Principal, Ballaugh naturally felt a curiosity about any achievements by his staff, and especially someone entrusted with acting for the university on the City of Culture Committee. *Nursery Scimitar* and the other one had to be treated as achievements regardless, so he'd given them some time. As far as he knew, the novels were not subsidized by the Arts Council or any other lot hatched to help loud lame dogs. A publisher had actually invested money in the works, and for that Maldave deserved recognition and a dip-into by Ballaugh. The publishers were small outfits, in Yeovil or Rotherham or the former Rutland or somewhere like that.

Now, still seeking insights on Maldave, Ballaugh turned to the piece in *College Collage*. It appeared to be a very short short story called 'See Overleaf'. Ballaugh read:

As tutor to a creative writing course, Osmond Vale received a lot of short stories and sketches from students. Generally, they were typed by request on one side of the page only. When pieces had been thoroughly workshopped in class and given his comments, Osmond would take spare copies home to his bachelor flat and use the clean sides of the sheets for scrap and drafts of his own literary output, avoiding waste: contributions could be fed into his printer so that they offered the blank side. Osmond was a prolific, even obsessed, author and got through a lot of stationery.

One July he sent off some new work to a publisher and almost immediately had an urgent phone call back from her. This was unprecedented. She jabbered with excitement and said one of Osmond's submissions captivated everyone in the office – 'but everyone, Os!' – yet it seemed incomplete and she absolutely must have the rest. The publisher started to describe the work she meant and to read out parts she found striking.

At first, Osmond was confused, then realized these extracts were not his. He soon grasped that by mistake he must have printed part of his final draft on the reverse of a student's contribution, and this workshop material was what she meant. In fact, she said that overleaf on the fascinating sheets appeared banal stuff – 'but I'm telling you really banal, Os!' – in no way related to the other, brilliant writing.

Osmond discovered a new aptitude in

himself: he could scream silently while holding a telephone. As the publisher went on quoting and rhapsodizing, Osmond remembered which student produced these words. It was Robin Maze. Osmond had always hated Maze for his creative potential, general flair, fecundity of projects, and insolence. Osmond decided to kill himself.

A few days later, the publisher telephoned again to see whether he could come up with more now. There was no answer. Luckily, she had his email address and sent a message. This said: 'Still thrilled by tale we discussed called SEE OVERLEAF, about dim tutor and accidentally included pages. At present, story still cryptic, leaving reader unsure whether tutor does kill himself in well-earned despair. Reply soonest.'

This made Ballaugh uneasy, even agitated. It certainly did nothing to soothe him. Could the tale be described as surreal – meaning deliberately unclear, arty, two-timing? All right, although he was an economist, he knew literature had to be allowed some skipping about and vagueness, but all the same he resented it in an anniversary issue magazine of this, his, university, and by one of his own staff. What did it say, this piece? Why did it have the same title as the story in the story? Why did Maldave write about a tutor in Creative Writing when he was a tutor in Creative Writing and, as far as Ballaugh could remember, lived alone like Vale? Hadn't Maldave been ditched by a woman?

So, did Maldave send stuff off to publishers on the back of pages containing work by his students? Had there ever been this kind of humiliating error? Did he have an obnoxious, smart student who wrote much better than Maldave himself? – not incredible. But Maldave hadn't committed suicide from shame and envy, had he? Ballaugh saw him at the *College Collage* reception, consoling and making up to that screaming, gorgeous-looking avenger, Lucy Corth. This kind of slippery, evasive, smart-arse writing did not seem suitable to Ballaugh for someone representing the university on the ECOC Committee. Ballaugh's already established doubts about Len Maldave really boomed now.

He left the bench and went up to his room. From there he emailed Mark Eider, a pal from his own undergraduate days, who had also landed a Vice-Chancellorship, but south

43

and across the border, in the University of Wales.

Mark, I'm under a tonne of grief here from staff problems in certain inevitably disfavoured departments, notably Creative Writing. You'll know the kind of greasy, jabbering, vain crew *they* are. Today while drinking drab white wine and *vol au vonting* I got called a cunt on account of Creative Writing Department turmoil by a girl named Corth, sweet smelling all over I'd guess, and constructed like a summons to excess. I wondered for a while whom to ask for advice and naturally I thought of dear old Mark Eider. I reckoned he must often have been called a cunt and would have built up a terrific file of possible responses. Plus, I have a chance here of hooking this dump to a City Of Culture dream but the lad handling it for us is a scribbling deadbeat and mystifier and his boss problematical.
   Any notions?
   Caspar

The reply was up on his screen within ten minutes.

44

Casp – had read about your place's en-forced sackings in the *Times Higher Edu-cational* and would have been in touch but to what purpose? I've absolutely no experience of anything comparable, I fear, despite your nice suggestion. Our Creative Writing staff and students are all gems – not effulgent gems, you under-stand, but happy, peaceful gems preoccu-pied by their tatty, wordy, often harmless impulses. Of course, it's the fucking poets among them who cause most grief. I wouldn't object if they were poets like Alexander Pope, who said, as you'll recall, 'Whatever is is right', because in our respective set-ups, Casp, you and I *are* plainly and incontrovertibly whatever is, and are therefore right. But the modern un-Popish poets have decided that whatever is is there especially to fuck them up, so they conspire and sabotage. I try not to employ them or admit them, though occasionally one slips through and mayhems sickeningly.

Mark

Three

God, that screaming attack by Lucy Corth on Ballaugh at the *College Collage* party – horrifying in a way, yes, but in another Len Maldave really loved it, enjoyed it, felt lifted by it. Emotion unvarnished, unmoderated – that's what an outburst of this kind gave, *so* spot-on for his stock of experience. He believed writers should feel grateful to witness the sudden upending of any sedate, orderly pattern, for example, the *College Collage* reception. Life did not supply many such genuine moments, but when it did ... when it did the author should observe, observe, observe, store, store, store.

And possibly more. Maybe one should occasionally go beyond simply observing the scene and filing away one's memory of it, like Wordsworth's damn lifeless 'recollected in tranquillity' prescription for composing. This meant all the rough bits and uncertainties and excitements might be smoothed out or ignored. Watching Lucy, Maldave thought that perhaps he should participate. He wondered, briefly pondered, debated inside. And then, yes, he knew he *must* participate. In some situations a writer should not stand aside passively and merely stare. This, surely, was one. Life took over. What he had to think was that it could have been he who got the Ballaugh chop if it weren't for membership of the City of Culture Committee.

Len went to Lucy as soon as she'd been persuaded down from that chair she'd stood on when flinging her tremendous, recriminating yells. A couple of reception guests led her to the side of the room and she stood near the doorway, weeping now. Len took her to one of the bars and tried to give comfort. This seemed to him an inescapable role, both as writer and man, and he never saw himself as other than each, overlapping, writer, man. Len went in for quite a deal of pondering the responsibilities of his role as author when seen against, or rather in conjunction with, his role as a man. Humaneness – he believed in that, always had. A writer had a duty to humanity, but so, also, did any man worthy of that title – the title, man.

Maldave realized the Vice-Chancellor probably wouldn't think much of him for seeming to side with Lucy now. Knowing

Ballaugh, Len guessed he would interpret the offer of solace as plain lust opportunism. 'Lay your grieving head on my shoulder, Lucy, dear, and then on my pillow.' This would be Ballaugh's crude, imagined scenario. He liked to be thought worldly, although an academic. But, again, whether as writer or man, Maldave considered kindness might sometimes rate higher than some mere back-the-boss habit.

Certainly, Lucy did add up to something very notable sexually. Even blotched by tears, her face had an animated, shapely loveliness. Most probably, few would associate such a winning face with cunt – not associate such a face with the insulting *word* howled, that is – the word shouted more than once at a university Vice-Chancellor from a grey stackable chair in plastic, though reasonably solid – well, obviously, it had kept her up there long enough to do the screaming. The animation always obvious in her features did suggest a spirited approach to people and things, however. Maldave wondered if, in fact, the word 'cunt' took on an added zing and deadliness when shrieked from those beautiful lips backed by radiant, but not dully regular, teeth. Absolute evenness in teeth Maldave detested. They made you think of orthodontics, not of the person.

The small irregularities of her teeth seemed to give the abusive word – abusive in this context, that is – a special, personal flavour; additional bite, as it were.

Maldave often contributed work-in-progress material to *College Collage* and had a possibly amusing squib in this issue, so it was natural for him to be at the anniversary reception. Of course, he knew where the original notion for that tale, 'See Overleaf', came from, but, in the way of art, he had transformed the bitterness into a kind of wry joke. He liked people to know he did playfulness, thematic oddity and sleight-of-hand in his writing, as well as the depth and seriousness of *Placards On High, Nursery Scimitar* and occasional poems. Graham Greene turned out many formidable, gritty novels, yet also gave the world lighter material, such as *Our Man In Havana*, which he called 'entertainments'. Len considered this admirable. Too much seriousness could look like pomposity. Pomposity Len ferociously despised. And then consider T. S. Eliot, so seminal and grave in *The Waste Land* and *Four Quartets*, but also able to produce his joky Possum poems, basis for the *Cats* musical. Maldave wondered sometimes whether, if he, instead of Eliot, had written *Four Quartets*, he would have called them simply *Quartets*, since to add *Four* must be a redundancy, if one were thinking of a quartet as a piece of music. Of course, a quartet could also be a group of four musicians, and in that sense one could have any number of groups or quartets, so to refer to four quartets, meaning sixteen people, then would be all right. But Len didn't think this was what Eliot intended. He regarded each poem in *Four Quartets* as one of those quartets and therefore the title must be verbose, surely. Had anyone ever pointed that out to the poet? How would he have replied? Alternatively, he could have called the poems *Four*, in the way that Brad Pitt film had *Seven* as its title. Or *Quartets*.

Len taught his classes to 'whittle down' their expression to 'the irreducable essentials'. He would speak such advice very forcefully and very often. He felt it crucial that students should take this lesson above all from him. His novels – *Nursery Scimitar* and *Placards On High* – were slim, neither more than 170 pages long, because of this 'whittling'. Plainly, he recognized that shortness itself did not guarantee a novel's worth. There was, in fact, obviously a valid place for what he light-heartedly termed for classes 'the fuller-figure' novel. Think of *War and Peace* or *Middlemarch* or *Dombey and*

Son, where thematic scope and sermonizing undoubtedly demanded many pages. Yet terseness did have its value.

He realized, though, that it could be regarded by some as absurdly arrogant to wonder – suppose time and other factors were different, and T. S. Eliot had sat in on one of Len's classes when young – whether on Maldave's advice he might have edited out that tautological 'Four' from the name given to his later works. Or, equally, he might have dropped the 'Quartets' of the title and simply called these works, 'Four Poems' or 'Four Reflections', since they definitely were reflective. Arrogant, yes, but Len had to admit he toyed with the notion. Eliot could easily have seen the silliness of his 'Four Quartets' label if he had envisaged poems called 'Five Quartets' or 'Nine Quartets'. In a class, Maldave would have used this kind of argument, known as *reductio ad absurdum* – taking things to their glaringly stupid ultimate – to persuade Eliot, the indubitably talented student, into a tactical rethink.

T. S. Eliot: occasionally Maldave also wondered whether he should have used initials – L. S. Maldave – rather than Leonard on his work. This might be regarded as a trivial point, but did initials suggest someone secure and unflamboyant about their merit and identity, and therefore more likely to impress publishers and readers? Might he have avoided some rejections if he'd submitted work as by L. S? Apparently minor factors like that did count sometimes. D. H. Lawrence, A. S. Byatt, P. D. James, B. Traven, J. K. Rowling – their success could be partly on account of initials, though the work did matter also, probably. He considered there should be two initials. Just B. Traven seemed raw and off-putting. So would L. Maldave. On the other hand, three or more initials would be wrong for a fictional work, suggesting a Civil Service kind of mind. On a factual, historical work it was probably OK, such as A. J. P. Taylor.

This sudden closeness to Lucy at the party was a surprise. He had expected the *College Collage* do to be just another campus function. By the time he arrived, it was going well, the room crowded and pleasantly noisy, plenty of white or red wine in plastic beakers from spouted cartons, and serve-yourself food on cardboard plates. Maldave did not mind these primitive touches. He liked to consider himself unfussy. When he thought later about Lucy's intervention he realized how easy it would have been for her to come in unnoticed among so many guests, take a chair from where they had been piled against a wall and in due course, once she'd located Ballaugh, quickly climb on to it. She must have spotted him in the scrum of people, then carried the chair to a spot nearer, so she would be looking down and directing her words unambiguously at him – unambiguously even if she had not used his name. Edging the chair through the packed room she might have become conspicuous, and was perhaps recognized; but by then it would be too late to stop her. Technically, of course, she had no right to be present once sacked from the university.

Oh, yes, sacked. That was the problem and what produced Lucy's splendid pain and rage. Maldave had watched Ballaugh's reaction to this brilliant, cunt-climaxing onslaught: the Vice-Chancellor's sudden half step away from her and then harsh tightening up of his lower jaw; the shocked pause of breath so his chest became entirely still for a few seconds; the single step, forward this time – not followed through – a single step towards Lucy, as if he meant to drag her from the chair and quell her. Maldave decided he might have to grapple uncompromisingly with Ballaugh and prevent such violence. This was when the urge to participate as well as observe reached Len. He regarded it as an important moment in his development as a creative artist and as a man – this recognition that life might now and then take precedence over art. The *College Collage* incident became for him a rite of passage, an emergence into a new maturity.

Ballaugh had a good appearance, for a university Vice-Chancellor – short, rather gross in the cheeks and neck, hair reddish and mostly gone, a flattish, porker's-type nose. Anyone in the least fair minded would guess he must have a brain and organizing ability to get a job and good suit like his, regardless of totally slob appearance.

Just before Lucy's statement, Maldave had his back towards her and the chair, talking to Amy Burdage-Pask, a successful local disco club owner whose place attracted students. She always bought advertising in *College Collage*. Of course, Len turned as soon as Lucy began declaiming her protest. For that initial moment, it made Maldave think of Luther nailing *his* anti-pope protests – ninety-five of them – to the church door at Wittenburg.

As far as Maldave could see, Lucy had no script or prompt card. The words simply came. Her voice was high-register but big enough instantly to quell all conversation in the room. As she bellowed on, Amy

Burdage-Pask whispered to Maldave: 'Brilliant, Len. This is staged, obviously. A "happening" as they used to be called. Wow, but wow! You university people! *So* brilliant. Showbiz manqués, most of you.' Until Lucy, she had been talking to Maldave about the City Of Culture campaign. Burdage-Pask was keen for the organizers to incorporate her club in their application portfolio's music section as 'High Street Small Hours Artistry', and wondered whether Maldave could put in a word through contacts at the Culture Committee.

'I'm on the Committee as Literature, Amy,' he said.

'Yes, I know. But if you floated the notion it might drift to where it mattered.'

'I don't know anything about the music aspect.'

'It's a decent, feasible idea, Len. As to the lit side, think of some of the utter shit they're touting. The "Edible Potted Epics" scheme – cakes from Wheaten Products bakery with *Faery Queen* and *Paradise Lost* verses in various icing tints. Is this going to bring the Culture title here? Those Wheaten bastards know somebody – somebody with campaign clout, do they? Cash has passed?'

Behind Burdage-Pask, Maldave spotted his boss, Basil Roffe, chatting to the editor of

College Collage. Roffe had one of what he called his 'designedly light-weight' poems in the tenth anniversary issue. In fact, to Maldave's surprise, because of Roffe's physique – middle height and very hefty – he composed good, cheerful and funny minor-key verse. An Anglicized Scot, he wore today a kind of Paris night-life apache outfit including black beret, tight white shirt and black waistcoat. There was a bold jokiness about how he looked, as well as how he wrote sometimes. Roffe could be unpredictable. He had fought Ballaugh very hard over the C. W. sackings – Lucy's and A. F. W. Ichbald's– but uselessly. He seemed to despise the City of Culture aims and wouldn't help. Occasionally, he seemed to despise Outreach as well, though he went along with some of it. Party guests moved about and, in a moment, the crowd obscured Roffe.

God, how terrific to switch from Amy Burdage-Pask's nonsense ambition to the solidity of Lucy's pain and rage. Oh, yes, yes, Maldave believed that any serious author needed communion with authentic pain and rage. By definition they had genuineness, they were life. Ballaugh must have known what was coming once Lucy began. He shouldn't have appeared so startled and devastated, surely. But perhaps he found it especially distressing to have the charges beating against him from an altitude, and from such a stupendous looking girl, person to person, in a room full of people he'd want the approval of. Then, of course, there came the forceful extra of those cunt references, given very precise pronunciation despite Lucy's inflamed delivery, perhaps improvized, perhaps popping unsummoned into her mind, and twice demanding utterance for their total, inspired, mot-justeness as she gazed down on him.

Possibly she had rehearsed her intervention at home – practised climbing on to the chair and arranging the main headings of her speech. But actual vocabulary, such as 'cunt', she would most likely leave to the inspiration of the moment, for rich immediacy; as with the 'unpremeditated art' of Shelley's 'Skylark'. Of course, Lucy could not be said to be addressing him from 'heaven or near it', as with the skylark, but she must be five foot six or seven, nearly as tall as Bas Roffe, in fact, though slimmer; plus the length of chair leg. Were the Press here? Maldave had seen no cameras.

Of course, much of the aggrieved stuff hurled by Lucy at Ballaugh now had already been seen in letters written by her and A. F. W. Ichbald, to the *Times Higher Education*

Supplement and other journals; also on a website. The accusations were: supineness by Ballaugh, acting as a Government creature in the hunt for foreign funds; haste in the sackings; monstrous casualness in the way dismissal took place – by phone from a Personnel nobody; seeming indifference by the university to work done conscientiously in the Creative Writing Department over several years for little money by Lucy and A. F. W., and by similar discarded teachers in other victimized departments. Her anger was personal and yet wide in implication, also, like Luther's ninety-five theses.

Free speech naturally rated high in this university setting even for someone no longer officially an employee, and at first nobody tried to stop Lucy's tirade at the party. Ballaugh had taken that single, possibly threatening, step but then obviously reconsidered. His shortness meant the step did not amount to much, anyway, Len thought, a little like a mallard's – and the Vice-Chancellor never came really close. When Lucy's address began to drift into repetition and sobs, Sam Oballe, a professor of English, Bas Roffe, and Charlene Essen, from the Student Union administrative office, moved closer to her. Charlene muttered something gentle and held out a hand to help Lucy down from the chair. Basil would be really concerned about her. Perhaps, like Maldave, he felt amazed that Lucy had been able to keep her balance on a not-too-stable chair, though jigging around in the excitement of orating, and occasionally sticking out a now-hear-this arm to point at Ballaugh and let him have the full contempt, no doubt some of it by proxy from A. F. W. Ichbald.

'Come, dear, this has been a strain for you,' Charlene Essen said to Lucy, still on her chair.

'For all of us, Charlene,' Basil said. 'Poor kid.' He could get very fatherly, although still only in his thirties. Maldave had never detected any sexual interest by Bas in Lucy, despite her looks and his possible claim through *droit de seigneur*. He could be charming, he could be dogged and hidebound. Lucy did not step down at once and drew away from Charlene's hand. It was as though Lucy trusted nobody in the university hierarchy after the injury done to her and to her work.

Sam Oballe said: 'I think you've given people things to consider, Lucy. Withdraw now? Leave them – us – to ponder. Look, strictly, I'm afraid you're trespassing. No right of entry to any university building, including the Union once your contract ended. You really should leave, Lucy. It's for your own comfort, as much as anyone else's. I make no judgement on what you said, but this was a brave act.'

'Yes, yes,' Bas Roffe replied. He began to tremble a bit, as if the strain really had damaged him. He bent his head forward in grief for a while. To some extent, Maldave would have liked to console him for the shrinking of his C. W. domain, but found himself committed by this time to Lucy. Maybe Basil felt ashamed that the protest had come from her, a fairly minor member of the department, not from him, its head. Probably, Basil had opposed the cuts in the university Senate, argued his doomed brief capably, wholeheartedly. A display like Lucy's might be no more effective, but it certainly had impact and drama, qualities so right for C. W. personnel, in Maldave's view. The beret sat there tight, like a dark reproach on Bas. He might be wondering why *he* couldn't have yelled 'cunt!'. As far as Maldave understood things, on no front did Basil Roffe have a comfortable time. His wife, a cartographer, worked abroad a lot. There were no children. Roffe went and sat down on one of the similar type plastic chairs lining the wall. He looked broken. In a while, Amy Burdage-Pask took the seat next to his and talked to him, perhaps offering comfort. Or she might imagine that even though Basil didn't sit on the ECOC Committee he would be able to influence his understrapper, Maldave, and get him to tout her disco.

'All right, I'll go now,' Lucy said. She ignored Charlene's hand and jumped from the chair, her face patched by tears but angled up, unregretful. Charlene and Sam Oballe walked her to the door between them, like bodyguards. Talk in the room resumed.

Maldave followed the three. 'I'll look after Lucy,' he told Charlene and Sam. 'We're friends. We've worked together.' He took Lucy's arm and they made their way to the ground floor bar. He bought brandies for both of them and they found a corner table. Lucy took a good sip and then began to wipe her face with a Kleenex from her jeans pocket. She gazed at him, her eyes still bloodshot from the weeping, but most of the dampness on the rest of her face now pretty well mopped up. Thank God he had decided to stand by her. Gazes like this – curious, sad, adult – did not come often to Len Maldave. Even when he and Elaine were together ... well, Elaine had been no gaze person. Adult, yes, but she did not believe in showing sadness, if she ever had any, and never seemed very curious about what went on outside her own special concerns; definitely not very curious about what Maldave thought or said – or wrote, of course.

'You needn't have come out, Len,' Lucy said.

'Now you're not a trespasser. You sit here as my guest. I'm still staff.'

'But you'll miss the useful people at the reception,' Lucy said. 'You might meet someone helpful – helpful to your work, I mean.'

'Oh, I hate flagrant pushing of self. A writer doesn't have to be a sales rep, I hope.' He felt that this statement did not quite amount to hypocrisy. He did regret missing the publishers, agents and literary editors at the party, though.

Four

Lately, Maldave found that whatever he might have planned for a class, the students always pulled discussion eventually back to Ballaugh's staff cuts policy. Some of them saw it as symbolic of a campaign against artistic and humanities subjects in favour of the practical, useful, employment-oriented courses. They feared a university could lose some of its traditional character under this treatment. Today, for instance, Len became tied up in that kind of discussion. Things started routinely enough, but he sensed change on the way. The shindig at *College Collage*'s reception would make awkward questions even more inevitable than usual. Everyone in the university had heard of it by now. He tried to ignore all that, but knew the class wouldn't.

Most years, as part of his general tutorial strategy, Maldave tried to show undergraduates that he was not simply a closeted and comfortable university teacher of Creative

Writing, but experienced the brutal side of the game also. To prove this, he made a practice of bringing in some of his rejection slips from several publishers and passing them around. 'You'll see it's a real heap,' he said. He considered the abundance crucial. A null plethora. A *Go Fuck Yourself, Maldave*, cornucopia. These brush-off bits of paper helped to what he thought of as 'de-iconize' him. He never spoke that word to them, fearing it would make him sound vain, as though he actually had icon qualities which needed moderating in case the students got scorched by their intensity and brilliance, the way people looked at an eclipse through smoked glass. But he liked 'de-iconize', considered it appropriate and, essentially, the very reverse of vain: he worked at humility, for heaven's sake. Such terse repulses from editors proved, didn't they, that he inhabited – and took bad knocks in – the big, cruel, deflating scene outside; was not a teacher in a safe seminar room fiddling over semicolons and half rhymes; or, this comparatively new development, an European City Of Culture Committee (Lit.) bureaucrap bureaucrat?

He felt what he deemed a caring duty to reassure his classes. After all, these were kids – undergraduates, but still kids – and a few of them might be nervy at taking on the course. That sexy title, 'Creative Writing', had worked its pull and led a good proportion of them to pick the module from a great bundle of university courses on offer. But perhaps some felt rather scared now. Overwhelmed. Only some. Most people who chose Creative Writing had ample confidence – some too bloody much – and no trouble with self-expression. This was an extra reason that lessons in the brick wall practicalities of a literary career became vital. He'd like to give them confidence, but not absurd optimism: taking a creative writing course did not of itself make them sellable, or even readable, creative writers. They had to develop stickability, endurance, and Len's plentiful rejections showed how he still needed and cultivated that quality, too, regardless of his undoubted achievements.

Of course, other university modules on the literary side offered their own immense range: 'The Anticipatory Sociology of Chaucer'; 'Shakespeare's Uncomedic Comedies'; 'Post-Modernism and the Suicide of Narrative'. Yet nothing could quite touch the scope in the title 'Creative', surely. The word thrilled many students. It beckoned them. Maldave would admit that this label, as half the name of a subject for study, did have a terrific, maybe gaudy, tone. Was it fanciful to claim that the first chapter of the book of Genesis and the Creation itself inevitably came to mind? When you got down to it, 'creative' could not be separated from the god-like – arrogant though this thought might appear; and certainly *did* appear, as Len knew well, to his colleagues, teaching Chaucer, Shakespeare or Post-Modernism. Mostly, they disdained C. W. and what they regarded as its pretensions, its glaring absence of scholarship, and foundation on utterly non-academic standards.

And then that term 'Writing' in the phrase 'Creative Writing'. Wasn't there an implied, soaring, proud boundlessness to this? Writing simply as writing – writing pure and *per se,* not the merely *applied, anchored, businesslike* writing as in essays about Chaucer or Shakespeare or the Post-Modernists. No, just writing, launching itself out and up and away from all the usual, workaday, practical *uses* of it – away from writing as no more than a tool or medium. This claim for the subject when spoken by Creative Writing tutors also caused lecturers on other courses to chortle or spit or both.

But, obviously, to the students who picked Creative Writing an instructor like Dr Leonard Maldave would seem intimidating, because of his intense, earned association with those very clarion notions, 'Creative' and 'Writing', plus his two published novels and several poems – achievements bound to awe beginners as, say, having McEnroe for tennis coach would, or Stravinsky as music teacher. Maldave wished to puncture this reverence. It embarrassed him. The lumpy file of rejection slips proclaimed, or seemed to, that even Leonard Maldave, member of the ECOC Planning Committee and author of *Placards On High* and *Nursery Scimitar*, poems and sketches, still had moments of failure in an otherwise sparkling literary career.

He certainly did not want to discourage the class by parading hurtful setbacks he'd suffered. Simply, he aimed to prove that despite his undoubted credentials he continued to battle the same indifferent world as theirs, a world where writers who sent their work out must not expect everyone at once to see its quality and intelligently rush to buy and publish it. Some of these kids might have rejection slips of their own. Empathy: he'd like them to know they could get this from him, never mind they were novices merely. Tolstoy had been a novice once. Maldave himself had been a novice once, oh, yes.

The rejections all related to one novel, *In Times Of Broken Light*, and were spread over eight years. Len regarded this book as easily his most impressive work, yet it remained untaken by a publisher. He would have considered it a cheap ploy to display all the refusals and then, as self-congratulatory pay-off, produce the eventual letter of acceptance, supposing there had been one. He often warned students against glib, enforced happy endings – told them how Dickens had chickened and provided two finales to *Great Expectations*, the original one tough and better, the alternative, soft and populist. Glibness Maldave felt entitled to be exceptionally severe on. And so this display of continual perverted fucking rebuffs for *In Times Of Broken Light*. Eternal.

He did calculate, though, that the class – like previous classes – would treat him sympathetically and conclude the refusals demonstrated faults in the ludicrous publishers rather than in his work. All publishers could think of was the millions sold by J. K. Rowling and Dan Brown. Len felt his classes would know about quality. After all, this *was* in fact the safety of a seminar room, not the big, cruel, deflating scene outside. He *was* the lecturer, and also Dr Leonard Maldave, City Of Culture adviser and published writer – *Placards On High, Nursery Scimitar* etc.

Always three or four of his most poised students opened any class discussion, and especially Vanessa Dale. 'It's like typical, isn't it, Len?' she said from up in her customary spot at the back of the room, a few of the thumbs-down letters now spread on the table in front of her. She stared at them as she spoke, something like revulsion across her face and in her voice. High grade sunglasses had been pushed up on to her forehead. She looked capable of commanding a tank squadron in the desert, and yet also of making fine points.

'Typical of what, Van?' he said.

'The whole charade,' she replied.

'Which?'

'It's an *industry*, isn't it?' she said.

'What?'

'Lit. Publishing. You send them your work – *In Times Of Broken Light* – tremendous title, full of unspokens, full of resonances, brilliantly inviting the reader in. But they say,' ... contemptuously she held up one letter, like a captured flag, and quoted from it, 'they say, "not quite strong enough for our list." I mean, "strong enough" – what are they getting at? Do they want a book or a weight-lifter?' She chose another: '"Buzzy,

69

topical book with a deliciously convoluted plot, but perhaps not a Magenta Press book, I fear." What *is* a Magenta Press book? Is there something especially Magenta-like or Press-like about a Magenta Press book? And "I fear". Do they *really* fear it? *I* fear – I fear they don't. This is formulae stuff meaning, *Stop bothering us, oik. Give us* White Teeth *or* Atonement. It's about marketing, isn't it, Len? Every book they take has to fit the sales profile laid down long before they saw yours, and a profile set by the past, not something new and adventurous.'

Maldave said: 'Well, yes, to some extent you—'

'I don't want to hog things or talk out of turn,' Vanessa replied, 'but, look, Len, you kind of *accept* this system, kowtow to it, don't you? Of course. You keep on trying with an undoubtedly great script because, because, BECAUSE – bottom line, you believe in how publishing things are run, regardless of this injustice and inanity. It's built in to your persistence. One of them turns it down, so you say to yourself bravely, patiently, "That's how the business operates" and decide you must complicitly, meekly, move on to the next. It reminds me of that super-crook, Hyman Roth, in *Godfather Two*. When something goes horribly wrong he says to himself,

70

"This is the life we have chosen", and so kicks up no fuss but moves on to the next project. And maybe you're right to do it like that. I don't know.' Maldave recognized the *Godfather Two* reference and didn't mind it too much. In the film, Roth was played by Lee Strasberg, a mighty figure in modern drama, and a creator of the Method school of acting.

Vanessa shrugged a while to signal honesty, impartiality, mere undergraduateness, as against Len's several rosy statuses. The sunglasses slipped down on to her nose and she shoved them back up. 'Look, to broaden things, we all heard of the deplorable developments at staff level inside Creative Writing here now, plus in other departments,' she said.

Maldave replied: 'Yes, not altogether good, but—'

'That *College Collage* disturbance the other day. And the Minister down here, sniffing around to see what's wrong in Creative Writing.'

'No, I wouldn't say that was his purpose at all,' Maldave answered. 'Probably the reverse. Congratulatory. This university is successfully following Government higher education policy.'

'You next to get the bullet, Len?' Vanessa

said. 'Bas, the prof, himself? Destruction? Chop, chop. Is this what a university should be about? This university – this department – does all the Outreach stuff fancied by the politicos, yet still gets kicked. Basil Roffe believes at least a bit in community as community – about people writing stuff for themselves, for reading to one another, just *expression* as expression, like a communal merging, a benign inter-invasion of people and cultures through writing. That's what the Minister wants, isn't it? So, Basil and others provide it, whatever his real opinion. OK, maybe – very maybe – what they do at Outreach sessions might get published. But not important. Not relevant, as the Minister sees it. Roffe the prof goes along. Yet still Ballaugh amputates. Why, Len? You went off with Lucy Corth, didn't you, after the *College Collage* bust-up?'

'Dr Ballaugh terminated the contracts of Lucy Corth and A. F. W. Ichbald, yes,' Maldave replied. 'This is not a secret. And there have been protests. That's no secret, either.'

'But, yes, look, Len, I *am* hogging things,' Vanessa said.

'Not a bit,' he said. 'I'm sure we're all glad to have a point of view put so—'

'It's hard to get an attitude to these rejection letters of your novel without knowing *In*

Times Of Broken Light itself,' Dave Merry said. He was about forty, in on a mature student scheme and now and then actually wore a tie. Maldave thought Merry might do a line in something snorted and strong more often than now and then. One nostril had become not too presentable. Funny, but quite a few folk always used the same nostril, instead of dividing the wear and tear.

'I don't really feel I could ask you to read the whole of *In Times Of Broken Light*!' Maldave chuckled. 'To summarize, though: it's about a strained, uncertain marital relationship. Some hints of menace. Much ambiguity.'

That arch piss-taker Huw Gance spoke from his front row spot: 'Do you know what I wonder, Len? I wonder if these rejections could be published as a short work in themselves. Pamphlet-style, unless you get a lot more, Len – enough to justify a properly bound volume. This would be a new kind of experience, yes, but admissible. Not a novel, obviously, yet a kind of ... yes, *anti*-novel – compare anti-hero – the rise of negativeness into an affirmative form. That is, the reader could amass from negative, even abusive, comments in these letters a notion of what the book must be like – or at least what it must be like when seen through the possibly

73

special minds – possibly corrupted minds, as Van says – the faulty minds responsible for these harsh snubs. We could deduce, infer, the system that produced such defective taste. We would not actually *have* the novel, and yet the novel would be a presence, a suggested entity, captured in a kaleidoscope of views, refracted to us. Title? *You've Read The Brush-Offs, So Forget About The Book.*'

Maldave had a notion that it was Gance he had in mind when writing about the repulsively talented Robin Maze in his squib 'See Overleaf' for *College Collage* and if it wasn't Maze it fucking ought to have been. Len said: 'I—'

'This sort of possible work – the collected rejections – would be comparable with, say, biography,' Gance said. 'Biography pretends to be a life. But, of course, it is not a life – the life in question might, in fact, be dead. We get critics talking about a *lively* life of, say, Aristotle or G. B. Shaw. Absurd? A biography is only a book, print on paper. The life is a presence, an implied entity, yet no more than that. Similarly *In Times Of Broken Light*, as represented in refusals to turn it into a book called *In Times Of Broken Light*, Len. The novel is present, imminent, inherent, and perpetually non-existent. Further, these letters are about the book but are also about the people and organisations they come from. This would be a reading experience on multiple levels. You might get a Doctor of Letters for it.'

Gance was the one Maldave thought might produce something brilliant, substantial, unkempt, difficult, hard- and paperbacked within five years. *Zeitgeist* baloney, the kind publishers fell over themselves for. The sodding broadsheets would bid themselves broke for serial rights. What sane student said 'Further'?

Vanessa held up another rejection note. 'This one calls it epistolary,' she said.

'Yes, letter-form,' Maldave said. 'A great tradition. *Clarissa*, Richardson's eighteenth century novel.'

'That's what I mean,' Vanessa said.

'What?' Maldave asked.

'Tradition. Lit. Are you stuck with that?'

'Surely emails have brought the letter back as a modern feature and it should therefore reclaim a place,' Dave Merry said.

'Certainly,' Len replied.

Vanessa said: 'So, *In Time Of Broken Light* is husband-wife conflict? This might be brill fiction, Len, but brill fiction as domestic interior, yes? Little sense of the capital O Other?'

'Which capital O Other is that, then, Van?'

Maldave said. He knew which fucking Capital O Other but felt inclined to force her to speak the idiocy. With any luck she'd get round to a pronouncement that to dwell on the thoughts of one or two, selected, fore-grounded, favoured characters, rather than on the community *as community* was '*bour-geois*', '*self-indulgent*', '*egomaniac*'. Oh, cliché, live for ever!

'Like that wider, societal element,' Vanessa replied. 'This is how the Minister and Outreach would regard it, isn't it, Len?'

'I don't know how they'd regard it. I want to know what *you* think,' Maldave replied.

Vanessa said: 'I see – visualize – a kind of traditional, hearty focus on what fiction obsessed itself with for so long, especially after the Romantics – the ego and mind of the individual. Is this like *bourgeois*, do you think, Len? The reader is required to voyeur into these letters and work out who's right and what's *really* behind the words each of them writes. No blame for that, but your story like presumes, as with those older stories, that such conundrums about the inner state of one or two chosen figures is worth the reader's devoted attention. All about tortured minds, troubled sensibilities.'

'Is it?' Maldave asked.

'What?' Vanessa said.

'Worth the reader's attention,' he replied.

'Some might query that,' Vanessa said. 'The Minister would argue that such writing preaches exclusivity rather than the totality. Is concerned with *bourgeois* introspection only, rather than the ... well, yes, societal, the communal.'

'*Bourgeois* again? What do *you* say?' Maldave asked.

'Is it ... well ... fair to ask what *I* as an undergrad think – an undergrad hoping to get up nobody's nose and come away with a good degree? We look at casualties like Lucy Corth and A. F. W. Ichbald and ... and it's like chaos here.' She sounded scared and desperate but still looked like a panzer commander. 'We're not sure what's going on.'

Five

When Ballaugh learned of this extraordinary new triumph by Lucy Corth he couldn't help a deep, very audible moan, though he did manage to cut it reasonably short. He was at home and someone from the English Department phoned to tell him, with plenty of detail, the vicious sod. At first, Ballaugh thought Fiona might not have heard his agonized reaction, but, after he put the receiver down, she allowed a decent, mock-considerate, wifely-care pause and then said: 'Another cataclysm, Casp?'

'Oh, nothing much.'

'You've gone streaky, dear – vermilion and white.'

'Oh, nothing much. It's that girl.'

'Which?'

'The one I kicked out with others as part of the required and therapeutic treatment of the university.'

'The beautiful one who called you a cunt twice, as what Mo would term the buzz has it?'

'There's an important booksy paper called the *Times Literary Supplement*, terribly strict and selective,' Ballaugh replied.

'The *TLS*, yes.'

'She's got seven poems in the current issue. Middle double pages. Fucking *seven*, Fiona. I'm told it's utterly unprecedented for somebody unknown. Usually, they'll print one, *one*, from an established name, or from a respectable published collection. But Corth – a novice bucketful. Think, Fiona: we end the girl's contract, among others, for extremely well-argued, fundamentally constructive motives, and now she's a fucking genius. This tin-pot, bottom-of-the pile university rejects her and then the smartest, most stringently selective metropolitan journal in the educated world takes her up and gives her—'

'Oh, Casp, you're going to look a right—'

'I'm told that if you buy the paper this week and just flip it open, not going through at a plod from front to end, just casually ruffle the pages, you'll most probably hit straight on the prestige spread of her stuff – much reverential white background spacing, the seven items, two of them sonnets, one, apparently, a so-called villanelle, such as all sorts of calibre people here and in France did in the past, including Dylan Thomas, who's had a lot of fifty-years-dead attention lately – all of it – villanelle, sonnets, whatever – under a big, beckoning head-of-the-sheet byline, "Lucy Corth".'

'Yes, you and Minister Maurice really are going to look a right pair of—'

'It might be just a blip.'

'Seven poems? In the *TLS*? A blip?'

He went to the office. Someone had placed a copy of the *Supplement* on his desk. The message was right: when you opened the issue it went naturally to this tastefully laid out collection of her verses. He gazed for an agonized while. Then, when he closed the paper, he saw that the back page contained a panel headed 'Notes on Contributors', and half way down came two paragraphs of biography, starting with the point that 'poet Lucy Corth (pages 13–14)' had 'until a recent breach with management' been a university creative writing tutor, naturally specifying which university. Both names, its and hers, came in heavy black, accusatory, look-at-me letters.

For a few seconds then, Ballaugh obviously thought, *A fucking conspiracy.* He saw devilishness, saw intrigue, saw much shit in flight and all flying his way. People had started gunning for him, had they? It could happen in this kind of job. Avengers for Corth, plus possible intrigue for the City Of Culture title. These published pieces were dum-dum bullets. Such malice would be standard among the literary lot. Didn't he recall reading in *A Quick, Humane and Human Guide to the Humanities* that Christopher Marlowe, famed as an Elizabethan playwright, covering all kinds of topics including royalty, had actually been knifed to death? So, how do you like these verse daggers today, Caspar Ballaugh?

He realized that what he had to expect now was Corth would be blitzed by bids from top publishers for a full collection of her stuff. This would be the next foul move: she gets a book of her verses produced by some top brand house and it wins every damn thing around bar the Nobel Prize for Physics. A renowned publishing outfit for poetry exists called Faber and Faber, so good they named it twice. Some firm like that might be after her. And, suppose – just suppose – suppose there was anyone in the world by then who hadn't heard she'd been flung out of Creative Writing here as superfluous, they would get it in the mass of fawning biogs of her sure to be launched. *A miserable, benighted alliance between the Government and a weak-kneed 'Vice-Chancellor' chief, Caspar Ballaugh, could have destroyed Lucy Corth's belief in her own brilliant talent, had she not recognized what cultural and personal negatives these two were – Government and university hierarchy. It is only natural that she should have publicly denounced Ballaugh in the kind of demotic, single syllable language that gives its characteristic tone to so much of her distinguished output.*

Meanwhile, although a business economist, Ballaugh knew the *Times Literary Supplement* had quite a worthwhile and world-wide standing. It would certainly get to all those spots already reached by Corth's and A. F. W. Ichbald's assaults through the Internet and the Press. It would reach every university and college, every library, the reading rooms of all those powerful London clubs, including the Athenaeum. Yes, this was your *real* sodding Outreach. The preposterousness of his position would be obvious everywhere – everywhere that counted. Goodbye peerage or even a mention in dispatches. He and the university looked arch twats, eternal twats: Ballaugh changed Corth's abusive vocabulary, but stayed with the same body area. People would probably assume he'd been knocking off Lucy and something went wrong between them. The *Sun* might come making inquiries, bribing students for gossip. Head teachers would direct their best potential students elsewhere. Even Mo might worry. That vast bonce could accommodate a lot of worry once he put his mind to it.

How had this been done, the malevolent Corth canonization through published verse? How? Influence. Whose? Ballaugh rang Sam Oballe and asked him to come over and speculate, advise. Sam had been around English Departments since Chaucer and could probably offer sensible views now. He confirmed, of course, that to get a poem into the *Supplement* really added up to something, normally, and to get seven in at one go was – his blunderingly hurtful words – 'near magical'. Oballe said: 'I doubt whether even Tennyson could have equalled this.' Ballaugh realized it would be more than a matter of decent rhymes and a steady syllable count. Anyway, these days, as everyone knew, a great number of poems didn't rhyme at all, but had qualities like 'self-awareness', and 'poise', and 'flexible authorial stance'. With the bulk of submissions for the *Supplement*, the editor most likely 'read to reject'. Balaugh had heard that phrase when, besotted by a previous partner, he agreed after plenty of argument to go to the Cheltenham Literary Festival with her, and one platform speaker – a well-known writer called Martin Amis – used this term about his own experience as a *TLS* editor. People in that kind of role expected nearly everything that came in front of them to be rot. The woman Ballaugh went with to the Festival had been a nice, literature-inclined woman herself, very kindly about his looks. He missed her now and then. Ultimately, though, she'd done the equivalent of reading Ballaugh to reject and married a farmer.

Oballe showed him which was the villanelle and mentioned its other recent users – a Theo Roethke, American, but also in the OK league, it seemed, as well as Dylan Thomas. Oballe stated there could have been no question of exceptional treatment at the *Supplement* for Corth simply on account of her face and fine body. 'This is no tit and arse paper, Caspar,' Oballe remarked. In any case, he said, if one were to presume sexual influence it would mean the poetry editor needed to be male and straight, or female and gay, and that s/he had seen and been within touching distance of Corth, which might not be so at all: possibly, Lucy just mailed her pieces in with a note, *Will this do?* The poetry editor's own reputation would be on the line for doing a splurge from an unknown like Corth, and s/he, plus probably the overall *TLS* editor, must have been authentically gobsmacked by her stuff. Yes, must have been, Oballe went indelicately on.

They evidently considered their *Supplement* had made a find and that this girl would be immense: 'Plath dimensions,' he suggested, 'or Emily Dickinson.' Oballe did not say the next bit, but Ballaugh thought it: the *TLS* believed this girl would be immense, regardless of getting dropped by Ballaugh's university, and possibly *because* of getting dropped by Ballaugh's university. He was bound to scent a scheme against him and the institution, and, beyond that, and obliquely, against the city's hopes in the ECOC campaign. Enemies and competitors would rush to ask whether, if the city possessed, and took pride in, a university pox-brained and addled enough to ditch this glisteningly talented poet, could said city ever sanely consider itself Cultural – a poet who could come out with villanelles? Ballaugh would be made to sound like Goebbels at the burning of the books.

In his trade as business strategist he was familiar with the concepts of chain reaction and chaos theory. An occurrence might cause further occurrences which caused further occurrences and so on, perhaps culminating in something infinitely greater and perhaps infinitely more damaging than the initial event. He wondered which *was* the initial event in this situation:

a. His decision to suck up to Mo and Government and embrace Outreach, in the hope of more Ministry funds at a tough time for university cash.

b. As another element in this cooperation with the politicians, the shrinking of some departments to allow the expansion of others – financially useful others, bringing money into the country from afar.

c. His decision to include Creative Writing and Corth among those for bashing.

d. His pathetic failure to consider that, with his sort of judgement, almost certainly one of the people fired would immediately turn out to be the biggest talent since Shakespeare.

Well, where it all started didn't matter a monkey's now. Ballaugh felt the approach of big disaster. It would home in on him. Sam Oballe left and Ballaugh went back to the *TLS* and gave a little more study to some of the poems. One featured a shot fox hung up on grim display in the countryside to deter other foxes. Should he find a subtext here? Was he, Ballaugh, being got at? He'd heard that his negotiating skill during a couple of university crises had been described as foxy. Another poem made fun of walking race

competitors – the comical, scrambling gro-
tesqueness of their efforts to get ahead. Yes.
It began: 'You numbered goons, why jig and
gasp and twitch?' Ballaugh's body had jerked
uncontrollably – jigged? – and he'd given a
brief, poignarded gasp when Oballe spoke of
Corth's achievement as 'near magical' and
probably beyond Tennyson. Also, Ballaugh
was aware he twitched now once or twice or
three or four times when he read about the
walkers' preposterous efforts to excel, and
about the gunned-down and humiliated fox,

   flung jackknifed on a barbed wire strand,
   as if he'd tried to leap the kale field fence
   and come unstuck. But not unstuck –
   well stuck,
   a minatory corpse, traditional.

Ballaugh felt he might be due to come unstuck. He knew what it was like to strive and
put himself about in goonish attempts to
succeed like those walking race idiots, even
with a place like this. Poems might be exactly
the method literary bastards would pick if
they wanted to rock him. That snotty cabal
never said things direct, but used slippery
metaphor, malicious allegory, evasive symbols, shady parables. The swine made a doc-
trine of double-talk, called it 'resonance' or

'evocation'. On one of his previous visits to Ballaugh's suite, Oballe had spoken of a work of literary criticism called *Seven Types Of Ambiguity* – had spoken well of it. That's how they were, these people. Nothing straight, nothing definite, nothing they could be held accountable for. Had someone spotted possibilities in Corth's jottings and 'arranged' publication as a retaliation for his supposed callous barbarism in reducing Creative Writing? Of course, Lucy Corth might have offered many more than the seven – seven poems, that is, not the seven types of ambiguity. Did some scheming avengers pick the ones most likely to mess him, Caspar Ballaugh, up? Was *he* the gloated-over wrecked fox,

> head tilted fractionally left,
> like upside-down contemplative?

Ballaugh straightened and tried to make sure his head was not tilted either way. Had *he* become a struggling, ludicrous prat in the university league table race, notable for what the walk poem called 'contorted, spit-wet lips?' He wiped his mouth with the back of his hand and met thick, warmish dribble. Removing it would not cancel the slurs, though.

Mark Eider sent an email from his campus in Wales:

Re the *TLS* spread, didn't I tell you to watch out for fucking poets, Casp? But I liked the one about her father's taste for long winded jokes, expecting them to 'do a full day's work/ Like waitresses or trawlermen.' A dig at a disguised you, daddy? Has she heard you in your interminable witty vein, then?
Mark

Not long after this, Ballaugh took a call from the city's Chief Executive, Elton Dape. Someone had told him about the *TLS*. Dape sounded urgent. He could do urgent very well. His voice stayed modulated, but jump-to-it modulated, familiar-with-power modulated. Elton was very big in local amateur dramatics, probably as a route to pussy – dissatisfied, older but not *too* old women wanting to 'find themselves', find themselves backed up against a wall in the green room. Elton had played major Congreve and Moliére leads. The Moliére had been in English, of course, but he knew a bit of French and liked to spatter it about. His urgency now came from more than theatrical skills. He meant it. 'Corth, Caspar. Can you get her back? You threw her out, but can you get her back? Actually born in *notre ville*, you know. This is a gift to the City Of Culture campaign. She's a home-grown celebrity, with glittering, mainstream recognition. Much stronger than the fact – if it *is* a fact – that Mrs Gaskell's cousin might have stayed at the *Goat* carrying part of the manuscript of *Round The Sofa*. Corths in the city go back to before tarmac. An ancestor had a job filling road holes to save coaches from disaster. He's in the archive, George Walpole Corth. This can be made a lot of, coupled with the girl's poems. She is *une véritable trouvaille*.'

'Bit late, Elton.'

'Tell her the sacking was a foolish slip-up, should never have happened.'

'It's the politics, Elton.'

'Politics?'

'In the widest sense. Governmental. There is a strategy here, you see. Emphases to be directed elsewhere, away from departments like Creative Writing, in the worthwhile interest of university health generally. Some adjustments were crucial.'

'I visualize Corth on our ECOC Committee. Definitely.'

'The Creative Writing Department already

has a representative on the Committee,' Ballaugh replied.

'Quite a decent lad, yes, I understand, but no real *name* to him, no *réclame*, nothing *vraiment étincelant*,' Dape replied. 'A girl like Corth – that kind of stature – you've heard of "street cred", well this would be lit cred and bound to enhance the application vastly. This girl has aura. I don't feel that with how's-he-called.'

'Len Maldave. Famed novelist, Elton. A muted quality, but quality just the same. Subtle. He's got one called *Nursery Scimitar*. It's regarded as definitely *au fait* with many a significant *thème*.' As to Dape's French, you gave back as good as you got or you'd get swamped in the *mer de merde*. 'Among *littérateurs* his kind of work is known as a *succès d'estime*, meaning not some vulgar best-seller, perhaps, yet valued by—'

'Yes, yes, I know *succès d'estime*,' Dape said. 'But from some obscure publisher in the sticks, Casp. There's a *hiérarchie* in these things – perhaps regrettably élitist – but so, all the same. By contrast, multiple publication in the *TLS has* to be a considerable matter. Her poem about urbanizing magpies, called 'On The House', I thought showed how profitably in touch with the seemingly ordinary, with the generally recognisable, she is, didn't you, yet able to transmute? In my book, that is the very *raison d'être* of poetry. I have the magpies one here as I speak – the way the birds peck at flattened cats on the road until they're almost hit themselves, "but scoot away, a chiaroscuro arc". How often one has seen exactly this when driving, Casp! I've sometimes mentioned it to my wife, that chiaroscuro arc.'

'What did *she* say?'

'Corth writes about cities, which is obviously very much *au point* from the campaign point of view, yet has also brought the city into touch with Nature as exemplified by the birds. This is an acute synthesis. I've always felt that one of the great impulses of art should be a wish to synthesize. Think of how *War and Peace* gives us the stupendous battle scenes and yet the personal dramas also. The title athrob with synthesis. This 'On The House' is the universal marvellously caught in a commonplace and even degraded incident – those "furred remains" in the road.'

As well as his synthetic reading, acting and French, Dape pumped iron and went after girls at amateur drams, in the office and afield. He'd probably heard of Lucy's physique. Of *course* he'd heard of Lucy's physique. That kind of flesh information had a way of getting about.

'She likes a bit of death,' Ballaugh replied.

'Ah, you mean the fox. But death is surely very much the legitimate realm of poetry, Caspar. Alfred de Vigny has a poem called 'La Mort du Loup', hasn't he – death of the wolf, its last words to us, "*Souffre et meurs sans parler*" – "Just suffer and die in silence"?'

'But it's *not* silent, is it?'

'I don't follow, Casp.'

'The poem's talking to us, gabbing at us, telling us to stay silent while we die, but he makes a noise about it in the poem.'

'Then Tennyson goes in a lot for death,' Dape replied.

'Well, yes.'

'Don't I remember from school, *In Memoriam*, page after page of it about the loss of his dearest friend, Arthur, and those yew tree roots invading the grave and bones? I gather a quite splendid chest, additionally.'

'Was Tennyson gay?'

'No, I mean the other poet's chest, Lucy Corth's. Isn't she rather gifted in that ... well, department?' Dape gave a friendly, apologetic grunt. 'Oh, look, you certainly don't have to tell me that the way she's put together and such concerns are entirely irrelevant to the Culture City Committee place. I know it. But I like to take the rounded view of people. Yes, a well-rounded view. Can you get her to come back?'

'Doubtful. In any case, *two* were fired from that department.'

'It's Corth we need.'

'There'd be a justified stink about inequity. A. F. W. Ichbald, who also went, would have a similar case for reinstatement. Or that's how their union would play it, and the Government still tries to give token recognition, even respect, to unions.'

'Is A. F. W. Ichbald neoned in the *TLS*, Casp? Poetry, the arts, are inevitably a discriminating game, not for the also-rans. The good get somewhere, the rest don't.'

'We're into Outreach here. We're *for* the people,' Ballaugh replied. 'That means a coolness towards individualism.'

'Take Rubens. Don't tell me hundreds of others weren't painting then. What happened to *their* work? Genius equals survival. And charmingly askew teeth, I gather. That always seems to signal amiability and good sportiness.'

'I don't know a lot about Rubens' mouth or ways.'

'I mean *Corth*'s teeth. You, personally, obviously couldn't approach her with an offer of a new contract. The buzz says she called you a *con*. At a public function. Twice. I don't know if that's true, Casp, and I don't ask you to comment either way. Twice. It's come to me from quite a few sources, though. If she did call you a *con*, and with an audience, which is what the reports say, one wouldn't ask you to forget that and invite her to return. I know you're not one to grovel, Casp, whatever the pressures might be. But perhaps some intermediary could go to her? Is there someone like that – *un agent honnête.*'

'She'd know I sent the messenger. She's bound to see it as a disgusting crawl.'

'Sometimes we have to cancel, or at least shelve, our pride, Caspar. We think of the cause. We're talking about Culture City here and the kinds of enhancement for all of us if we succeed. Obviously, the city campaign will be projecting Corth, anyway. Whether she's working for you or not, she remains *natale*, descendant of a locally established family, and is a star writer. But it would be a broadening of her significance if we can put into our bid-papers that not only is she of impeccable pre-tarmac lineage here but contributes to the current life of the city through the university. A job would anchor her with us, Casp. The danger now is that some other outfit – a rival university – might want Lucy Corth on their staff for kudos. She'll pull new students. That hate poem in the *TLS* about her father and his ghastly, lumbering jokes – this will get to many kids, really bring fellow-feeling. My own father's jokes were like it. Courts would accept them as extenuation for murder. I wouldn't be surprised if Oxbridge come sniffing for Corth. I can imagine my own Cambridge college in the rush. They'd say "Stuff Outreach – Outreach is for the birds, and the provincials." When I go back occasionally for gaudies, dons there are still pissed off Auden went to Oxford as professor of poetry, even though most of them think Auden was rubbish, of course. They won't want to miss out on Corth, too.'

Well, stuff Oxbridge, likewise. 'There's Maldave,' Ballaugh said.

'What?'

'He seems close to Corth.'

'*Vraiment intime?*'

'He went to her instantly after some unpleasantness at a function in the Students' Union. She was weeping, having made rather an unfortunate display of herself.'

'Is this when she called you a...?'

'And then disappeared with her,' Ballaugh replied.

'Naturally. When they're upset it's often a way in. One hand to wipe away tears, the other to reach their soul, and so on. Kindness surprises them, destroys their guard. They want to say thanks, the dears. They feel they can't do that adequately at a distance and in their garments. Twenty-four, twenty-five, Casp? That's a sweet age to catch them tearful and at altogether maximum emote.'

'But it's smelly, isn't it, Elton?'

'What?'

'To ask Maldave to speak to her. Then, if she comes, we replace him with her on the ECOC. "How'd you like to cut your own throat, Len?" Not very honourable, I'd say.'

'This is a business situation, Casp. With your training, you'll surely understand that. The market. She is scarce, at a premium. We must think of Oxbridge very likely moving in on her, Casp.'

Yes, fucking Oxbridge. 'I'll mull over Maldave,' Ballaugh said. If there were conspiracies against him, he'd better start conspiring himself.

Six

In the early days, soon after Outreach had begun to get modish, Ballaugh used to go occasionally to a workshop put on by Basil Roffe or members of his staff under this banner, sometimes accompanied by Fiona. These were evening sessions off the university campus at venues around the city and for the local public. Generally speaking, a Vice-Chancellor did not sit in on a class held by one of his subordinates because this could look oppressive and a threat to academic independence. But these extramural gatherings came in a different category. They were, above all, community events and, as Mo and his father would gorgeously put it, for the people – all the people who turned up – Outreach outreaching. Ballaugh felt entitled to drift in, virtually as another member of the public. Whoever was leading the seminar had always seemed pleased enough when he or the both of them showed.

Now, Ballaugh told Fiona: 'You know, I'd like to go back to one of Roffe's Outreach conclaves. I'm damn confused.'

'You do still seem bad, Casp. Pressures? Looking at you, I recall Blair and the way Iraq and that Bristol flats scandal and the BLIAR T-shirts got at him – the geometry of his face gone skew-whiff, his eyes like they belonged to someone else. Now, darling, although I'm sure you haven't become any shorter, you *seem* shorter. Things have begun to close you down, love, compare the Incredible Shrinking Man. Sometimes, when you come into the room I want to cry out with relief and pleasure, merely because I haven't failed to spot you, which could be hurtful. Your nose has widened, as if you need more air to keep going, given all the problems.'

'My training – not at all right for this kind of situation.'

'Which kind?'

'I'm an economist. I'm used to precisions, predictablities – one way or the other.'

'They promoted you. They think you're more than mere graphs and data tables. They believe you can deal with all sorts.'

'Do *you*?'

'Mo obviously believes in you.'

'Do *you*?'

'Is it about this Corth broad?'

'She's a star,' Ballaugh replied. 'Suddenly, a star. The university needs stars on its staff. Think of that big critic with initials and an open-necked shirt at Cambridge.'

'F. R. Leavis? They treated him like a nobody.'

'Yes, but a star nobody.'

'Downing College. *Downing*.'

'Here, the City Of Culture Committee must have stars. Literature is about stars. Only stars survive. Ask Elton Dape. There's an item called quality. It's necessary and Outreach might not have much to do with it. I think Basil Roffe feels that, but he does Outreach because Outreach is policy.'

'Dape mentions Bulwer Lytton, does he?'

'Who?'

'Writing at the same time as Dickens, just as popular, now forgotten.'

'No, Dape talks about the people in Rubens's time, but who were not Rubens. That's a fair number, obviously. They don't seem to rate, not like Rubens, anyway. Dape's hit something with that logic. It would be mad to argue against him.'

'Same as Lytton.'

'There you are.'

'Mo wouldn't like the idea of stars. He's for *the people*. And *you* didn't like the idea of stars – those Fellowships at All Souls.'

'But are stars *necessary*, just the same?'

'Soccer stars are necessary if you want to fill a stadium and get TV to cough for the broadcast rights. Pop stars are necessary if you want to fill a rave field.'

'I used to think there was something in Outreach, Fiona – I mean something beyond modishness, and populism, and the Government money that backs it. I did. I did. A noble, democratic, anti-privilege notion.'

'And Lucy Corth has changed that?'

'Possibly. She gets seven poems in the *TLS*. Not many of the people as people can do that. I'd like to remind myself why we have Outreach. What it stands for. I know the theory, of course. I have to *feel* it, though. Feel it again. I checked: there's a workshop at the Seawall pub this week.'

'I'll come.'

'I hoped you would.'

'Poor Casp. I've heard bits, but what exactly does she look like?'

'Who?'

'Corth.'

'Why?'

'If she's a beauty, will you seem an even bigger idiot for letting her go?'

'Her looks are not relevant.'

'No, they're not relevant, but they count.'

'Do you think one of Mo's or Basil's Outreach groups will produce somebody who gets seven poems in the *TLS*?'

'Not the objective. They aim to show the community how to represent itself in writing. That will do. A completeness.'

'Yes, and this *is* worthwhile, isn't it?' he replied. Ballaugh spoke passionately. 'I used to be almost sure of that. Perhaps I still am sure of it. Yes, perhaps.'

'I don't know. Those people you mentioned just now were the community,' she said.

'Which people?'

'The ones who were not Rubens. As you said, that's quite a few. In fact, most.'

'Right.'

'Nobody remembers them. They communed with each other and were a community. They *don't* commune with us. We do remember Rubens, though. *He* communes.'

'That's because he painted pictures and we have them.'

'Other people painted pictures. They were not worth remembering.'

'Who says so?' Ballaugh asked.

'Us. Or people like us across the centuries.'

'Is being remembered important?'

'Dape thinks yes,' she replied. 'As you just said, Cities Of Culture need names. Some of the names will be old – old and remembered: "Matthew Arnold slept here." "Rubens slept here," – if only he had. Some of the names will be now-people who look as if they'll make it. If they make it, they might get remembered, too. Cities Of Culture depend on them, as well.'

'Some colleagues, including Roffe, hate the whole Cities Of Culture notion.'

'Naturally.'

'They see it as what they term "league-table vulgarity". Call it "jumped-up monkey shit". They refuse to sit on any City of Culture Committee. Our very off-Broadway novelist, Len Maldave, will do it, yes, but what does that say about the Committee's worth?'

'Monkey shit can't jump. Monkeys can.'

'Outreach doesn't care about mixed metaphors – all those grammar and syntax worries. Just expression as expression from people as people,' Ballaugh replied. 'Writing should capture what's seen as their "folk power". Impact is the aim, not careful prose.'

'Dape is after impact, too, for his City Of Culture campaign, isn't he? The city's application needs impact, or it won't be noticed. Think of how London secured the Olympics for 2012. They didn't achieve that by having their apostrophes in the right place.'

'Outreach's kind of impact is different.'

'Which kind is it?' Fiona asked.

'Communal.' Ballaugh recalled that to dub something or someone 'common' had been one of his mother's most ferocious insults, much worse than 'dirty' or 'evil'. She probably wouldn't think much of 'communal', either. Did her influence still reach him a little; at least a little? He could think of moments when he felt quite baronial in Vallin Court: really savoured the place – its size and stateliness and history and separateness from the streets of the city. From the community? Its non-Outreach? Its *anti*-Outreach?

'Isn't Basil's wife away a lot mapping?' Fiona said. 'That might push him towards the community and comradeship regardless of what he thinks of the policy.'

They arranged to attend the next Outreach evening session. Ballaugh went to the office and during that afternoon sent another email to Mark Eider in his Welsh haven:

Looking for more advice, pray. Multi-pressured. Fiona says it's as if I'm physically dwindling on account of all this and she's scared I'm becoming so shrunken she might step on me by mistake, like a beetle. Recap scenario follows:

104

1. I arranged the sacking of Lucy Corth and A. F. W. Ichbald from Creative Writing, among other redundancies.

2. I am made to fret about that when Corth turns out to be a poet one rung down from Dante and, therefore, on the face of it and more than that just right as an inspiring Creative Writing teacher.

3. Common sense and Elton Dape, the city's chief executive, with overall responsibility for the City of Culture campaign, say get her back at once regardless – regardless, that is, of Mo-driven Government thinking.

4. The City of Culture campaign, if successful, would do me and the university much good.

5. I was appointed to do the university much good.

6. I would like to do myself much good.

7. I could make preparations for reclaiming Corth (and for fairness A. F. W. Ichbald) by considering an approach to a C. W. teacher, Maldave, who might be close to Corth and could deliver and broker the proposal. He snuggled up consolingly to her after that famous little pother here.

8. But, Mo Theel more or less said on his visit that the most constructive stroke I ever pulled was to chuck Corth and Ichbald out.

9. He would probably declare this achievement grew, and notably grew, when Corth called me, exclusively, a cunt. It proved I must have balls. (Excuse the jumbled genders.)

10. I am deemed Mr Outreach and Mr Outreach is loved by all in Westminster.

11. Mr Outreach may, in fact, become Lord Outreach.

12. This would seem to depend on Mr Outreach remaining faithful to his tenets, the chief one of which is Outreachism.

13. This faithfulness might be regarded as destroyed if I seek to bring back Corth and Ichbald since Mo believes they were ditched in a fine cause – solvency of this place.

14. Corth is almost sure to get more publication and more kudos and to all normal thinking folk – ie, folk unconnected with Mo or the Government – I will, as things thus evolve, look even more an inveterate Philistine twerp.

15. What the living fuck do I do, Mark?

Eider sent a reply, though not one that dealt properly with any of Ballaugh's fifteen points:

Following his call on you, Mo Theel, our dear Minister, did a visitation here, like one of those all-powerful French Revo. Deputies on Mission in the Terror. He was radiant with praise for your Outreachery and fanatical de-élitism. He believes he will rise further in the Government – ie, join the élite – by touting élitism's opposite. Also he'd noted Fiona. Be alert to this, Casp. His enormous, jargonizing brainbox – you wouldn't want him sliding that great, comical cube down into warm recesses which should be reserved for you while mouthing *inter alia* his slogans.

Mark

Ballaugh enjoyed the Outreach session a few evenings later. He'd known he would. Or he enjoyed matters until that sudden, surprise contribution from Fiona: a surprise to him, that is; the rest of those present seemed to take her offering as natural, cheerfully making a discussion topic of it. They appeared to understand her better than he did. Ballaugh felt shaken; realized that, if things went on at this rate, he would soon get very used to feeling shaken and forget what it felt like *not* to feel shaken. The incident seemed to echo a story he'd come across not long ago by

Somerset Maugham. Ballaugh read a decent amount of fiction, but what he called 'traditional' fiction, not all the brain-ache, make-weight stuff around these days where tales wondered about the nature of tales, and about gristly, shifty topics like identity, truth and what he gathered was called 'closure' – ie, should books have endings, since Life itself did not; and, if books didn't have endings, what should they have, so they could be fitted between a pair of covers and get featured in display bins at W. H. Smith's? The Maugham piece was called 'The Colonel's Lady'. Suddenly tonight, because of Fiona, Ballaugh saw himself as like the Colonel. God, identity problems! Perhaps he should be in a story.

Outreach did have something. Of course it did. He'd never thought otherwise. The question had to be, though, whether it had as much as Mo and his mates believed – plus those above and beyond Mo. Outreach offered ordinary people the chance to present their thoughts, their hopes, their backgrounds. Surely nobody could dispute the worth of this, not even Elton Dape. Outreach gave a voice to those who previously had no voice. True, it could be argued that the bulk of these voices had more or less bugger all to say and said it at appalling, tedious length and with sensational clumsiness. But then, think of the length of some novels by George Eliot or Thomas Hardy, or *Paradise Lost*.

An elderly man distributed and read aloud in the stick-at-it, fluting voice of age, a poem about being taught as a schoolboy during the Second World War how to kill tame rabbits for food and so supplement the meat ration.

The cony took it in good part, stared out
with innocent urbanity upon
this classroom full of boys who'd come to see
our history master do the job – a skill
more useful now than groaning on about
Wat Tyler or the Heights of Abraham.

Ballaugh could see that this belly-based, small canvas approach to history had a place, and a good one. Wat Tyler and the Heights of Abraham mattered, but so did school food clubs in 1942. After all, this old creative writer had survived the war and reached the present – reached a state-of-the-art Outreach meeting – with his poem, by eating the subject of it. In the final verse, an older boy who'd been conscripted returns on a visit and gratefully reports

that during unarmed combat
training he'd been taught the way to kill
a Jerry with one swift downward blow
against his neck, sidehand used like an axe.
He'd found the history master's lesson with
the rabbit put him quite a bit ahead
of all the other conscripts on his course.

Yes! Oh, yes! The sudden widening of subject. Valid. Effective. Chilling. Outreach could reach out and reach back and produce something, no question. But Lucy Corth could produce too, and what she produced reached an audience bigger than this Seawall meeting. And did it rate higher than what they heard at the Seawall? Deep. Too deep for Ballaugh to reach. He was an economist, not a literary umpire.

'Irony,' an elderly woman in the group said, announcing herself according to procedure here as Edith Cater. 'I love it. Irony's not just something for the professionals, the established, the taught. It's built in to all of us. The whole literary bag of tricks – irony, hyperbole, litotes, pathos, wit, the lot, all those polished devices – they're all as natural to any human being as toes or sweat. We, here, in our workshops have only to release them, freeing eagles from a cage.'

Eagles, cages – so Outreach *could* do metaphors that added up. Discussion began on what was irony. Another woman, Beryl Vitone, said she'd always understood it to be saying one thing and meaning the opposite, like if someone farted aloud in church and the vicar broke into one of his prayers to comment, 'Charming.' Edith thought this might have a *whiff* of irony to it but was mainly sarcasm, a rougher commodity, but still valid. Where exactly did the irony in this poem come, Beryl asked.

'At the end,' Edith replied.

'Which part?'

'The former pupil, now a soldier.'

'What's the irony there?'

'The by-product.'

'Which?'

'Lessons in killing a rabbit unintentionally teach him how to kill a man. There's a deadpan wryness to it,' Edith replied.

'Did you intend deadpan wryness, or cooking pan wryness, Eric?' Beryl asked the poet.

'Deadpan wryness was one of my objectives,' he said, 'although I didn't set out with the precise intent to do deadpan wryness. To some degree it came unbidden. A poem can have many objectives. Think of the *Ancient Mariner*.'

'What does it mean, "deadpan"?' Beryl replied.

'It means the poet does not tell us direct that this is deadpan wryness but in a wryly deadpan way leaves the reader to find the deadpan wryness for her-himself. Or not find it,' Edith explained.

'Or *not* find it?' Beryl asked, astonished. 'Excuse me, did you say "or *not* find it"?'

'Oh, yes,' Edith replied.

'So, then, what if the reader *doesn't* find it?' Beryl said.

'That's the thing about irony,' Edith replied.

'What?'

'The reader might not always spot it and takes what is written as straight. Newspapers don't let their staff use irony for that reason.'

'If the reader doesn't spot it is it there?' Beryl asked.

'Not for that particular reader.'

'So, would the deadpan be *too* dead?'

'This is the beauty of deadpan,' Eric replied.

'What?'

'Subtlety, ambiguity.'

'I heard there are seven kinds of ambiguity,' Beryl said.

'Seven, seventy, seven times seventy,' Basil replied. 'But, yes, there is a critical work called *Seven Types Of Ambiguity*. Rather old hat now, perhaps.'

'Old hat how? Why hat, anyway?'

'If someone wrote up this conversation and put it in a book would they mean it as irony?' a bimbo-type asked, giving her name as Ro Pale, short for Rowena.

'Ah, that's the post-modern, self-aware approach!' Basil cried delightedly.

'Who, me?' Ro replied.

Other discussion concerned the type of animal. One work-shopper – Ted Sutton – knew in depth about keeping rabbits and thought the one killed by Eric's history master in 1942 would have been a mongrel. Big Flemish Giants had plenty of meat on them but also large, unpromising bones. The answer? Mate Flemish Giant does with black and white Old English bucks, smaller but potent. The young produced had a combination of both parents' assets: ample flesh, economical skeleton. Beryl, who'd been interested in a definition of irony, said this seemed the opposite to what happened in some European royal houses where, because of in-breeding, offspring inherited double doses of their parents' frailties. Was it ironic that simple rabbits could be made more useful by their parenting than great aristocratic dynasties? But Ted, the man up to speed on rabbits, said they should not be regarded as simple. Rabbits could display intelligence and marked individuality. In the same way, he objected to the phrase 'innocent urbanity' in Eric's poem. He believed it suggested that the rabbit might stay urbane, unworried, too dim and innocent to realize butchery came next, despite finding itself in a classroom surrounded by gawping boys, and with their history master close and tense and plainly not interested in Wat Tyler or the Heights of Abraham now. Ted referred to a rabbit that showed great fight and independence in *Women In Love,* the D. H. Lawrence story, and to a series of major American novels where the actual hero was called Rabbit. Although not wishing to get pedantic, he thought the term 'cony' meant a wild rabbit, not one hutched.

A different woman, Lois Simpson, wearing a heavily tasselled poncho and with an unlit cigarette between her fingers, said that if the rabbit *were* a so-called Flemish Giant, this might be symbolic, because Flemish meant Belgian and Belgium in 1942 lay subjugated by the Nazis. It seemed heartening that this small, occupied country could nonetheless supply nourishment – *gigantic* nourishment

– to Britain beyond the meagre meat ration, helping in the fight to resist that very Nazidom and eventually defeat it. Poems often spoke in symbols, particularly animals and birds, such as the albatross in the *Ancient Mariner*, mentioned earlier, and even a wasp in E. M. Forster's *A Passage To India*, spared from a squashing and thus a symbol of the sacredness of life in all forms, although an apparent pest.

'Symbols I can do without,' Fiona said. 'I like to tell it what I term "glimpse-wise".'

'Well, right,' Basil replied. 'You have something for us?'

Fiona and Ballaugh were sitting at a small table with their drinks in front of them.

Ballaugh said: 'Oh, no, Fiona doesn't—'

She stood, took a sheet of paper from her handbag and unfolded it. She'd come here prepared? At none of their other visits had she tried anything like this. 'It's called "Procedure",' she said and began to read, her voice gentle, unpushy:

A public scrutiny rubs
random regions of my flesh
when turning up for dates with you
in bars.
It brings me rosy moments,

early on, before I've even hit the gin and
french;
or advocaat in honey,
for a saint's day change.
You're never near the door;
and so I brave the distance: viewed –
without malevolence or balefulness –
by banker-types and managers of
franchise shops nearby, in Warburton Street
itself,
quite possibly.
You're on a stool, unmoving,
like a Hopper nighthawk,
and knowing it, of course,
though trilbyless.
You slowly turn,
as in a Hopper picture someone might,
and via a very spiky whisper
just for me, inquire:
'Why is it you give every cuff-linked sod
in here the eye, you moistened bitch,
when strutting through, and gift them
extravenously
your by-the-bucket forearm scent?'
The mirror's huge, lit from below.
It shows him gaudily unradiant,
those neck-folds sticking eight years on his
age,
which was already bad enough.
But he's here,

he's here, he's here,
and obviously on time,
in laced-up shoes that match.
We get back to a room,
not pissed exactly but, from feel,
I couldn't tell you to a centimetre
where my nostrils end and lips begin.
He's right, as usual:
yes – and when we settle down
to it again, I miss the social milieu
and sound of coughs and money chatter
in the bar: our Friday twosome loneliness;
the sheets experienced but spruced.

Because there seemed to be no rhyme, Ballaugh had to guess at the line-breaks from the way she read and paused and read on. He thought the poem might be in that form he'd heard of which was no form, *vers libre*. Free verse. Yes, fucking free. Free from tact and decency to him, free from modesty and compunction, stuffed – stuffed! – stuffed with curt mystery. She never met *him* in bars. An Indian woman with a denim jacket over her sari provided no name but said she liked 'cuff-linked'. This was metonymy, in which one – or in this case a pair – of particular items represented something much more; as a British execution used to be referred to as 'the rope'. '"Cuff-linked" suggests a kind of man – the banker types and franchise bosses having an after-work drink in the bar, perhaps in custom-made shirts with hand-stitched holes for links. Presumably the man waiting for her on the stool has no cuff-links, as well as no trilby, and this causes his bitterness towards them and jealousy. Although clearly inside the bar, he feels himself to be an un-cuff-linked outsider. He is obsessed by forearms – his own not ending in cuff-links, hers, he believes, tickling up males with scent as she walks from the door towards him.'

'This is a poem about hope,' Ro said. 'Oh, such brilliant hope, such inspiring hope!'

'Franchises in Warburton Street itself are, indeed, notoriously pricey,' Beryl said.

'Hope from its title onwards,' Ro replied. ' "Procedure." Procedures are necessary. Consider the procedures laid down for evacuating a stricken submarine. Procedures get us to where we want to go. Automatic. Efficient. The procedure gets *them* there, to between the experienced sheets – meaning many others have used this bed for a grind before them, because they had a procedure, too. It's a folk procedure, a fuck procedure, probably extra-mar, naturally. These two – all right, he snarls like misogyny at her, but

118

he hasn't stood her up – he's here in tripli-
cate – and he's early. Possibly a druggy or
alco, but tonight he's coordinated his shoes
OK and even done them up. She and he can
make it, make it, make it. It's routine, but it's
also fresh – the sheets "spruced". This is
eternal renewal, symbolized in laundry.'

'A love poem but anti-romantic,' Basil
said.

'I'd say romantic,' Ro said. 'He'd probably
find it easier, quicker, to get naked because
of buttons on his cuffs, not having to struggle with links, especially if he's got the
shakes. He could just push his shoes off, no
unlacing, probably. Men do that when in a
hurry to strip.'

Nobody seemed to expect a comment
from Ballaugh. He wondered whether Fiona
had taken up with a poet, suppose the man
at the bar in what she wrote knew about the
metonymy of cuff-links. He tried to remember if he'd noticed her regularly absent on
parts of Fridays and smelling of experienced
sheets, though spruced, when she got back.
Was this poem biography or fiction, or both?
He would not ask. It might seem naive and
unliterary, the kind of banal, plodding approach a business economist could fall into.
Did Fiona do gin and French and/or advocaat? Did she come back with one or other

on her breath? Which saints' days? At least the man hardly sounded like Mo, supposing the Mo-ness of Mo had any consistency and established shape.

In the Somerset Maugham story, the Colonel, a cliché figure – narrow-minded, Rightist, vain – is appalled when his wife publishes a volume of love poetry, very graphic and passionate, and describing a flat stomach definitely not his. Jealous rage grips the Colonel, but when he reads the poems thoroughly he finds the lover has died. Just the same, the Colonel remains furious and hurt. He wants to confront his wife about the affair. He consults a solicitor friend who tells him to do nothing, accept it, or his wife will leave him. And after a lot of bluster and threats the Colonel takes the advice. He can't contemplate life without her. Then, though, comes the typical, sharp, cynical Maugham pay-off, a turn-around: the Colonel, who's been reduced to prolonged panic by the possibility of losing his wife, says he doesn't understand what the lover could conceivably have seen in her.

But Ballaugh understood what any man might see in Fiona, perhaps even more so now she'd turned poet, even if only an Out-reach poet at present. This would be especially true of a man who looked eight years older than his birth certificate through neck fat; his birth certificate nearly a no-no, anyway, quite apart from the neck fat.

Seven

When Maldave looked back to events right after Lucy's special shout at the *College Collage* party he saw something really good developing between her and him. Of course, her success a bit later on in the *Times Literary Supplement* brought big, all-round changes, but those moments with the brandies just after the party remained meaningful and golden for Leonard. The rapport would endure, wouldn't it? Frequently, he thanked God that he (Leonard) went to comfort her and was not content merely to do the author bit and remain detached from events; nothing but a voyeur spectator looking for copy. Such elegant detachment of the writer was what John Keats called 'negative capability', and this probably meant something once. But in the immediate, post-chairborne shriek period, Maldave sensed he must not fail Lucy.

Naturally, he already knew her quite well, even before the *College Collage* sequence.

They worked in the same department, or did until Lucy's departure. He had admired her from the first days she arrived at Creative Writing; admired what he glimpsed of her which, though, was not all that much. She came in, always carrying a green canvas briefcase, did her teaching, then disappeared. He might bump into her in a corridor or the Senior Common Room, and that would be about it: as a junior member of staff she did not attend departmental meetings. Len's novels, his classes, the City Of Culture responsibilities, rather preoccupied him and, stupidly, he had been short on attention to Lucy. Possibly, bad difficulties at home with Elaine around that era might also have distracted him. Perhaps he was off women. Perhaps, also, he sensed that someone with a face and body like Lucy's must be already nicely fixed up in a relationship. Elaine's attitude and voice had knocked some confidence out of him. Actually, Maldave found out subsequently that, like himself, Lucy was in the aftermath of a relationship. Such brilliant luck!

In the ground floor bar, with the drinks before them, Lucy had said: 'Obviously, in a way, it's unfair to attack only Caspar Ballaugh, as Vice-Chancellor. With more time, I would have got on to university policy altogether.'

'People will understand, I'm sure.'

'That's UK university policy, not merely here. Ballaugh is only an example. There is something generally rotten and/or clumsy in the system.' Lucy took a good sip, then brought a Kleenex from her jeans pocket and began to mop her cheeks. 'Did you find my carry-on outrageous, Len?'

He felt proud to be consulted by her, even if it was too late for advice to matter ... 'You're hurt. Understandably hurt.'

'The onslaught on Ballaugh – cruelty? Suddenly – suddenly, I don't know, he looked so small and fragile and bald-stroke-ginger – so *pathetic*.'

'Ballaugh? He *is* short but would seem especially so because you were up on the chair and are, in any case, tallish for a woman. A different viewing angle,' he said. 'Remember Harry Lime in *The Third Man*, gazing from high on a Ferris wheel and seeing people at ground level like ants.' Or compare Hemingway, trying to end Fitzgerald's Zelda-provoked worries in *A Moveable Feast* by telling him that glancing down at one's own cock when naked would make it seem smaller because of perspective. But Leonard thought this might not be the time for that reference.

'A. F. W. Ichbald, I'm sure, would never have demonstrated as I did, Len.'

'Reactions to such situations cannot be standardized. People vary – and thank heaven for it, Lucy. There is a fullness, a variety, a diversity to life and to character.' Oh, hell, he knew he could often fall into sickeningly pious guff when talking close up and gravely to a woman with excellent tits.

'You see, I loved the teaching, Len. I learned so much. It was such pain to have it taken away. A part of me is gone.'

Maldave had tried to make big facial signs of sympathy with this bollocks and murmured in quite a stricken style, 'I know, Lucy, I know,' as if he, too, loved the teaching and would be devastated to lose it. Actually, though, he longed to ditch all sodding teaching and get to his novels and stories full time. *Nursery Scimitar* and *Placards On High* had both been small-house published and cost him money rather than made it, so he knew he would have to put up with students like Huw (Boobytrap) Gance and Vanessa (Rommel) Dale and their successors for a time yet, and perhaps for keeps. He had hoped *In Times Of Broken Light* might do the trick for him, and so his approaches to commercial publishers with it. But all this produced so far was enough rejection slips to sustain dangerous, satirical discussion in his classes. 'You say you learned from the under-graduates, Lucy, but I'm sure they learned much more from you,' he stated.

'Minimal. I'm not like you, Len, an established author, someone who has only to walk into a lecture room for the students to sense experience, accomplishment, craft.'

At the time, pre-*TLS* and her warranted beatification, Maldave experienced a real, wholesome compassion for her when she said this, and a need to de-iconize himself again, as he did with the students. Reputation could become an embarrassment, a divisive bind. He didn't want a Dr. John-son–James Boswell relationship with her. So fucking right! When they spoke that day after the shindig, she'd had a few poems publish-ed in regional magazines and come third or fourth at a Midlands literary festival com-petition. He realized that, yes, to her he must seem a recognized, substantial, indisputable, daunting talent. Such status, he'd admit, brought a duty to help those just trying to start, and he believed he would feel this about any novice, not just someone with the beauty and natural warmth of Lucy Corth. He had yearned somehow to give her access to that status, a share in it, as mighty trans-port planes brought rice and agricultural

126

machinery to famine areas. This did not then amount to a sexual urge. Not at all. Or not entirely. Len would have regarded it as disgustingly opportunistic, even degenerate, to attempt something of that kind from his special position when she was so distressed and momentarily weak. The girl needed mentoring, not sneaky, heartless seduction.

Maldave had decided he must bring her into contact with the sort of literary work which showed most clearly his efforts and his ambitions. It would help her, allow her a borrowed solidity of achievement. To do that, though, he must not go to volumes already published. This would surely seem smug and the kind of self-regard he despised and tried to escape by using his rejections of *In Times Of Broken Light* for undergraduate inspection. It was a book he still considered his best and potentially the one that would 'break him through', as publishers' jargon had it – though, so far not about Leonard Maldave. However, he had faith in it, and such faith now extended to the wish to give Lucy Corth a sort of beneficent therapy from these pages, a unique lift to her morale. 'You know, Lucy, you remind me of a character in one of my books.' He'd almost said 'works', but caught himself and strangled this boom-boom.

Immediately, she brightened, as if terrifically flattered, he thought, as would be inevitable. Evidently, she assumed the character concerned would be 'good'. He liked that. It showed she knew he admired her. 'Len, that's wonderful, a privilege. Which? Do you mean the woman who returns the bankrupt snail farm to profit in *Placards On High* by flair and doggedness, although wholly ignorant at the start of all to do with snails for kitchen use?'

'Not the precise circumstances of your life, Lucy. Jill – my character – is married. You're not, are you? Not partnered?'

'This is *such* a compliment, Len.'

'What?'

'To see me as like one of your creations. But it's unnerving a little. As if ... well, yes, as if I've suddenly taken on an extra personality. And I know it will be a full and entirely credible one because of your fine skill at characterisation. Your people are people.'

He heard an unconscious echo of Mo here. 'The book's called *In Times Of Broken Light.*'

'Marvellous, teasing title.'

He said: '*In Times Of Broken Light* is unusual in method. I'm having a little trouble placing it with a publisher, as a matter of fact.' Yes, very much as a matter of fucking fact.

'Inevitable. Publishers fear experiments. They want last year's bestsellers rehashed.'

'Unusual in method for now, that is,' he replied. 'Actually, a return to one of the oldest forms of novel writing.'

'Oldest? You mean letters? This is *so* exciting, Len. I've always admired the letter form. Absolutely straight from the soul of the main characters, no intervention by the author – though of course, it *is* the author making up the letters! Tell me what I'm like in it!' Her face still shone with real pleasure. He would have put fairly big money on its genuineness – up to a tenner. 'Or, even better, I'd like to see the script. It's not in your briefcase, is it?'

'At home.'

'Oh.'

'We can go to my place, if you like.' There was still nothing sexual to this, he could swear. It was not the grossness of 'Come up and see my etchings.' He had a task, that's how he saw it. The girl needed rebuilding after injury and stress, and by bringing her into involvement with his writing he might help. The face, breasts, hair, sweet breath, crotch-clasp jeans – none of it at this Good Samaritan juncture was especially relevant.

'Go now?' she'd asked.

'Why not?'

'But, as I said, you'll miss the useful people at the reception,' Lucy replied. 'You might meet someone with the guts to try out a new – or old-new – type of novel. There are a lot of people present from London or Berlin or New York who might have come specifically to find you in your hideaway! I don't want to—'

'I'd sooner forget them for now.' Another aspect of the cure he sought for her was to remove Lucy from the Ballaugh-university environment and into surroundings where an author daily struggled for creative progress; rather like taking a soldier from the dirt and din of battle and giving him rest, cleanliness and quiet in a monastery. 'Yes, we should go now and you can see *In Times Of Broken Light*. I've had my drumstick and plonk at the party. And I don't think they'll let you back in to get yours, suppose you were entitled. I can give you coffee or another drink.'

'If you're sure.'

He had felt *half* sure. She was right and if he stayed he might run across someone useful he could talk to, cajole, plead with, about *In Times Of Broken Light*. Improbable, mightily improbable, but, yes, a chance. And

Ballaugh would possibly not feel so resentful, and therefore spiteful in the lecturer promotion stakes, if Maldave seemed to keep his time with Lucy brief – just a sort of token gentlemanliness to relieve her troubles. 'Come on, we'll go at once,' he said. 'I feel a kind of compulsion to bring you and Jill together.'

'Intriguing.'

At his flat they took armchairs facing each other in the living room and drank coffee. The place probably looked much too damn tidy, but there had been no opportunity to rough it up. He did not want her to label him as domestic and house-proud now he lived by himself. That would be creepy. He was an artist. But did this amount to more cliché thinking, brought on by breasts at – metaphorically – and only metaphorically – hand? Why shouldn't an artist's place be orderly? His work required order. His setting, too?

'It's about discord between a husband and wife,' Maldave said. 'Discord moving towards violence. Dennis, Jill.'

'Sounds powerful. Elemental. Could you read me a paragraph or two?'

God, try and stop him! 'It's Jill writing to her mother,' he said, and began:

My dearest ma,

I would have replied sooner but – well, Dennis is in and out of the house at odd times and I don't feel safe with pen and paper. It's all right this afternoon. He's definitely gone to town and I'd hear the car early enough. I'd still argue there's a lot to be said for Dennis, as long as you make allowances.

It was lovely to hear your voice on the phone recently. Nobody speaks my name in quite the loving way you do. But please don't ever say anything ... I mean anything DIFFICULT. There are three extensions here which make it unsafe, and we are all the time plugged into a recording machine that clock-logs any disconnections, and he would want to know why, wouldn't he? Damn crazy, really, isn't it – all this brilliant electronic stuff for communication by phone makes it necessary to use olde-worlde letters!!! Mobiles? Don't trust them for security. Remember Prince Charles and Camilla! Email? Don't trust it for security.

Just think that previously people used to write stories – whole novels – entirely in letters, like that play from the book, 'Clarissa', on TV, Lord knows how many instalments. Those days, they really took their time getting raped!!! Well, I hope nobody ever makes a book out of <u>our</u> letters, mum!!! In his little way, he often reads.

Glancing back over, I don't know why I said I don't feel safe. I'd hate to give you worry. Safe is such a <u>major</u> word. I don't think he would go beyond, not in a <u>major</u> way. My feeling is, deep down he's yellow. In any case, I'm careful not to antagonize. I do things absolutely as he wants now, more or less, and he can really be quite sunny. Well, obviously!!! This was the side he used to show. I know I could still love him, KNOW IT, if only he would stay like that for a little while. There are these sudden falls into – well, call it turbulence.

Yes, of course, OF COURSE, it would be fine if you came to visit. Don't worry. He'd be fine. Yes, September or October, fine. I don't keep your letters – so they'll never make a book!!! It's wise not to have them in the house, given his filthy rummaging. I read each in the neighbour's house where I asked you to send them – as less dodgy than to here. Alice is a real gem, or 'Care

of Mrs. A. V. Ward' to you when you write!!!
I bought her an azalea. Alice leaves me
alone in her sitting room with your letters
for as long as I like – tea and croissants.
Lovely.

'Etcetera,' he grudgingly ended.
   'Oh, I can see it!' she cried. 'Yes!'
   'What?'
   'The resemblance.'
   'To you?'
   'The up-and-down elements – sometimes
full of jokes, sometimes into fear. The tussle.'
   'Attack Ballaugh one minute, blame your-
self the next.' He'd only said Lucy reminded
him of Jill so as to get her here and talk
about the script. He longed to give her a distraction, a balm. But if she immediately confirmed resemblances he'd back her up.
   'Can I see the whole thing, Len?'
   He handed her the typescript. She skim-
read for, say, fifteen minutes, sampling pages
right through. He watched her for reactions.
'It's been around a bit, has it?' she asked.
'Dog-eared.'
   Lucy sounded suddenly very brisk and
businesslike, no longer tearful or disturbed
over what she had done at the party. She
startled him. The voice was the voice of a

professional.

'I *have* sent it out a few times, yes,' he said.

'Is this the one I heard of from one of the students? You showed them the rejection slips?'

'I thought it necessary and fair.'

'Incredibly modest, I'd say,' she replied. 'A heap of very terse, very blank rejections, I gather.'

'A number, yes.'

She re-scanned a few pages. 'We need some sex,' she said.

Oh, yes, yes, Lucy, yes.

'I can see it has fair narrative pull, capable characterisation – as I'd expect, credible, measured analysis of a disintegrating relationship,' she said. 'Effective opening, satisfactory end, but between I sense a lacuna or two, and perhaps that's why it has failed, so far. I don't suggest just sex chucked in as a saucy extra. Not even necessarily graphic. But nonetheless explicit. Integral. Fleshly. That's what I seem to miss, fleshliness – fleshliness that, pardon this, Len – fleshliness that fleshes out the tale, a tale already passably strong but needing the glint and smack of excited skin.'

All right, she could come out with 'lacuna', meaning, obviously, a gap, and this could be regarded as a proper literary term, but to hear her call for a sex flourish in the book had dismayed him. 'Excited skin!' And, God, he had been prim about Hemingway and Fitzgerald! Actually, it had dismayed him quite a bit that she should do other than regard the typescript as blessed by integrity and skill, or at least pretend she regarded it like that, at this stage. Instead, this shit sandwich: 'OK at the start, OK at the end, but in the middle...' He grew almost angry for a few minutes. After all, she was nothing but a small magazine poet and competition runner up in zombieland, kicked out of a novice job as very dispensable – last in, first out. A shock to hear her talk commercialism. She claimed the opposite, of course – not sex as a 'saucy extra'. Yet, what else could it be, if wilfully tacked on to a work already complete? She referred to the proposed additions as 'integral'. How was that conceivable if the book at present existed without it and without *her*? And it *did* exist, constituted, in Len's view, a valid, viable, whole statement, not to be messed about with, tarted up, by some very unproven kid.

'Sex?' he said. 'Well, I—'

'She mentions that greatest of letter books,' she replied.

'Richardson's *Clarissa*?'

'Exactly.'

'I don't think my work is—'

'What's the theme?'

'Of *Clarissa*?' he said.

'Sure. Well, she actually speaks of the theme, doesn't she?'

'It's—'

'Sex,' she said. 'A massive novel all about sex. What somebody called the core of all best-sellers, "procrastinated rape".'

'V. S. Pritchett.'

'Probably. The letter form is absolutely *made* for sex, Len. Its characters putting themselves on a plate. One can feel the frustrations, hear the gasps.'

'Well, I—'

'Let me think about it, will you? I'll take this away with me, all right?' She waved the script. 'I've an investment in it, haven't I, if you feel I'm like Jill? And the title. Yes, it shines. But, but ... I don't know. Florid?'

'I'll give you a lift.'

'Thanks but the bus will do. I can read some more *en route*. I look forward to that. I've got a pencil so I can write in additions where I feel your stuff sags.'

Although Maldave saw no cameras or outside Press people at the *College Collage* incident, someone must have given the local paper a tip about what happened and next day a girl reporter had called on him at his room in the university: just arrived, no pre-phoning. 'You'd better talk to Dr Ballaugh, the Vice-Chancellor, and Lucy Corth herself,' Maldave said.

'We will, of course, but I gather you went off with her at the end. She sort of wound down with you, didn't she? The bar? Brandies? Then exit together? I've had a word with *College Collage* people. Are you two close, you and Corth? Soul mates? More than that? We'd like your account of things, obviously. You're what we term "a prime source" – not a participant, at least until subsequently, but one of a few brilliantly placed witnesses.'

Maldave had liked this. He enjoyed the idea that this little, gimcrack, sheltered, academic room should have a Press reporter in it, even though only provincial; and should have a prime source in it, also, the prime source being Leonard Maldave. And, of course, this prime source had a novelist's rare gifts: he could observe with consummate and sensitive accuracy, he could register the shifting tones of an occasion and imply their significance – imply, not crudely, laboriously, hammer home an interpretation. Yes, this reporter showed tactical nous in coming to him before seeing Ballaugh and Lucy.

But he thought it right to keep things clipped and rationed, all the same. That was how a scene like this ought to be played. Prime sources did not do their prime sourcing in a gush. They had control. Don't chuck that position away by gab. Prime sources one-lined, and often with one-liners which told next to nothing. Discretion. Tact. Opaqueness. A prime source must play it so. Enigmatic. This journo could guess – *had* guessed his unique value, but could not *know*, and would not be told, exactly how much of a prime source he really was. Through involvement with *In Times Of Broken Light*, Lucy Corth might be regarded as part of him now. A grafting had taken place. She was in possession of his typescript, and this contained his hopes, his driving force, and so much of his selfhood. And because of resemblances to one of the book's characters, Lucy might also be seen as sweetly linked with him. Could a prime source be more prime? 'At the time, she seemed distressed,' he said.

'Other people could have helped her.'

'Other people did.'

'But it was you who stuck with her.'

'I got some brandy for Lucy, as you say. Talked some calmness.' This phrase, absolutely spontaneous, he adored. It did all sorts, making him sound like a rock, yet also considerate, empathic and seasoned, as if he had often heard a sacked university staff member scream cunt from a stood-on chair at the Vice-Chancellor, and felt the best and well-tried follow-up to be calmness. Often his ability to encapsulate a mood or condition of things in a few spot-on words amazed him. He would not be aware of calculatedly selecting them. Yet they came to him from a wonderfully ready, deep store and would be startlingly right. 'Yes, talked some calmness. That's all,' he said.

'Someone told me you left the campus with her, she blubbing still, but near recovery.'

'I thought she shouldn't be alone in her state.'

'No, I can see you might think that.'

'What do you mean?'

'She a looker, yes?'

'She needed support.'

'Are they going to drop on you for that?'

'Who?'

'The uni authorities – cuddling up to a flagrant troublemaker. Couldn't be *more* flagrant, could it?'

'I don't like that phrase.'

'Which? She has to be seen as a trouble-maker, doesn't she – would *want* to be seen as a troublemaker.'

'"Cuddling up."'

'Your bosses won't like you siding with her, openly siding with her. Will they come gunning for you?'

'But that's not at all how universities work,' he'd replied categorically. No?

'How *do* they work?'

'Meaning?'

'I gather Corth had been fired – like out of the blue fired. Why?'

'You must ask the Vice-Chancellor about that.' He prized this hand-off: brisk, rich in protocol.

'Well, naturally. But what do *you* think?'

'You see, the Vice-Chancellor was appointed to take this new university forward. A specific task.'

'Forward how?'

'Ask the Vice-Chancellor.'

'A *big* shake-up?'

'Universities and their departments continually evolve or we'd still be discussing how many angels can dance on the head of a pin,' Maldave replied.

'Discussing *what*?'

'An old-time topic, when universities dealt only with religion and tried to bring it within the scope of academic discourse.'

'Who decides how?' she'd asked.

'How what?'

'They evolve.'

'The need for change is accepted by everyone as a given. Needs become apparent.'

'Government pressure?'

'People are appointed to judge the temper of the times and act in accordance.'

'Which people? Ballaugh himself? The Minister was down here lately wasn't he, doing some leaning and arm-twisting, checking on implementation of higher ed. policy?'

'An Education Minister naturally takes an interest in education.' Maldave had felt almost sorry for her then. She might not be used to wit. She sat in front of his desk, a tape recorder on her lap, though she made notes as well. He'd been to the dispenser and brought coffees for them both.

'So Corth and Ichbald didn't fit any longer? Why?' she asked.

'Ask the Vice-Chancellor.'

'She's really is a bit of a cracker, isn't she?'

'Who?'

'Corth. You banging her? This sort of writerly thing between the both of you turning into something else? Plath–Hughes precedent. Did Ballaugh fancy her himself, sort of *droit de seigneur*? Is that's what behind it? Nothing to do with education?'

Absurd, but Maldave had liked this, also.

142

The reporter seemed to accept it as obvious that women would want Len. He wished Elaine could have heard the questions and seen the sexual value put on him. How about this reporter's reaction, her *personal* reaction to Maldave? Did *she* respond? He found her a bit dumpy, but good skin, lively eyes, intelligent bra. Maldave felt interestingly attractive. He said: '*Two* people were sacked.'

'Ichbald as cover. Ballaugh couldn't let people see it's all about thwarted sex, could he? This is a bohemian sort of department, isn't it? Has to be. Rackety behaviour the norm. Writers are like that. Think of Graham Greene.' The comparison had delighted Maldave – Greene turning out tremendously significant religious stuff like *The Power And The Glory*, and at the same time shagging in all directions, no conscience. 'Rackety.' Yes, things in a creative enclave *ought* to be rackety, he thought. Or rackety as measured by duller, non-creative standards. She said: 'I suppose Ballaugh couldn't stand it. That the trouble? If he couldn't have her, he'd make sure she wasn't around for *you* to have.'

'We run respected degree modules in Creative Writing. Nothing "rackety" about them.'

'And why did Corth attack only Ballaugh, not go for the whole Government attitude to universities?'

143

'Ask her.'

'My understanding is – she sneaks into the *Collage* festivities, takes a plastic chair from a stack, carries it through the crowd, climbs on to it when she's near Ballaugh and abuses him, the chair grey or possibly blue. Facts. We live on detail in our game, you know. I also spoke to Amy Burdage-Pask, the disco owner. She gave me a description of events. I gather she chatted to you. Smart piece. Are you doing something there?

'The *College Collage* party very quickly resumed its proper tone,' Maldave replied.

'How do you know? You'd left with Corth.'

'I'm told.'

'She called him a cunt, didn't she? Twice. Top of her voice. This would seem to indicate a personal, maybe sexually-based, resentment rather than policy.'

'You can't put that in the paper, for God's sake.' Some of Maldave's steeliness broke up.

'I need to know. Sometimes we need to have more than we actually publish. In any case, we've got asterisks.'

'Asterisks?'

'We're a family paper. "Cunt" would be printed as C. asterisk asterisk T, or possibly C asterisk, asterisk, asterisk. I think most people could work out what was meant.'

'Really?'

'Or we could say "made a reference to female genitalia", or, then again, "pudenda" which is generally the female, I think. Can you confirm she called him a cunt twice? I have it from Amy Burdage-Pask but we like two sources, same as Woodward and Bernstein in the Watergate tale.'

'I don't see what she said as so important.'

'An indication of the bitterness. Particularly saying it twice. Obviously, actually to have yelled "female genitalia" or "pudenda" at him couldn't have had anything like the same force. We'd broaden out from her outburst to comments on the staff relations in the department and in the university generally. And on the abysmal frailty of untenured university contracts these days. There's a real industrial relations theme here, dramatically highlighted in the cunt references. This is the way journalism operates – moving from the seemingly slight matter to the general. How do I describe you?'

'Describe me?'

'If I quote you.'

'As saying what?'

'You're *Dr* Maldave, aren't you? Lecturer in Creative Writing. And author, I gather. Sorry, I don't think I've heard of your books. They're called?'

'*Nursery Scimitar, Placards On High.*'

She made a note. 'And what are they like?'

'Like? They're novels.'

'Like J. K. Rowling? Jeffrey Archer? Colin Dexter? Or, Greene, as already mentioned. You R. C.? You're on the City Of Culture Committee, too, aren't you? This kind of thing could damage Elton Dape's case a bit, especially if some of the national papers pick up the Corth intervention tale. Local university in turmoil. A pity. Some of the London Press don't give a monkey's and would spell out cunt plain both times, though not in headlines. Reading a word like that is the kind of thing to stick in the minds of Culture competition judges. Where did you go after you left the campus with her? Your place? Hers? The tension got you right horny? Both?' She drained her coffee. The action had drama to it. 'Hey, look! —something I've just thought of: did the two of you actually *plan* her performance, as a joint thing? You helped her against the establishment? That's a terrific tale. You got together and said, "The *College Collage* occasion will be exactly right for the protest," – the way people put on demos at political party conferences. You coached her on the cunt references – where to work them in for maximum smack? What is she anyway?'

'Who?'

'Corth. Why did she have the job? I mean, you're a novelist, up there with Graham Greene and Micky Spillane, so everyone can see why you're wanted for Creative Writing and the City Of Culture Committee. But Corth?'

'A poet.'

'A poet where? Slim volumes?'

'Magazines.'

'Oh.'

'Prestige magazines.'

'Which?'

'Several.'

'Who says so?'

'What?'

'Prestige.'

'These things are pretty generally recognized.'

'By?'

'People who know.'

'Which?'

'Consensus,' he had replied. 'In the creative-stroke-literary field she's been noted. She'll make a real stir any time now. Oh, yes, any time.'

'Who says?'

'Consensus.' This scoop-merchant had referred to possible jealousy in Ballaugh but Maldave wondered whether the girl herself felt some of that about him, Len, the poor, unsatisfied thing. On arrival she had given him her card and he glanced at it again now. *Rebecca Heston, Senior Reporter.* Did she resent his apparent championing of Lucy's poetry, especially if Heston thought something went on between Lucy and him? A poet might appear a tough rival to someone who churned out here-today-gone-tomorrow hack news stories. Yes, again Len felt sympathy for her. She seemed clever and would probably realize the chasm that existed between what she did and what true creativity was. She acted brassy but probably suffered a conviction of deep inferiority in his presence, and when talking of Lucy. Of course, Rebecca Heston would be even more crushed if he told her that Lucy and he were working together on one of his novels, an unmatchable, entwined intimacy. Yes, unmatchable. The thought made him pause, made him realize he possibly shouldn't be sizing up Heston as a sexual prospect when he and Lucy had the beginnings of what might be a brilliant, all-round relationship, both being solo for now.

She said: 'Obviously, we're in favour of the City Of Culture campaign. It would be good for the paper – increased advertising, crowds of visitors, general prestige.'

'Absolutely.'

'But as a responsible paper we can't down-play a story like this just for the sake of the C. of C. bid.'

'Why not?'

'Too many people know about it.'

'If too many people know about it, why tell them again?'

'You tit-fixated?' she replied.

'What?'

'You stare. It's a sort of compliment, I suppose. Corth's nicely breasted? I'm gay, though, you know.'

'Immaterial to me.'

'Yes?' Heston stood and went to the door, as if leaving, but when she opened it muttered, 'Bert, now,' and a photographer had stepped into the room and took four or five photographs before Maldave realized what was up. She'd said amiably: 'Well, listen, Dr Maldave – we've got those, regardless. But now, would you like to do a couple of poses? You might come out looking better than in the snatched versions. Do you justice, as far as can be.'

'It's mad,' Maldave said. 'I'm only inci-dental. What do you want pictures of me for?'

'If it turns out to be a love triangle. I've got to speak to Corth and Ballaugh. That's what

I mean.'

'About what?'

'The posed pix. You've got to be made to look as though you could pull a woman despite competition from your chief. Do him right profile, Bert, will you? The other one no – too like a tooth abscess. And not front-on, either, Bert. Dodgy. We're going to do our damn best for you, Dr M.'

Heston's report did appear in *This Morning*, but simply as a straight and cleaned-up account of the Lucy–Ballaugh incident, with no suggestion of a sex aspect, no picture of Maldave, no asterisked four letter word, and not even a reference to female genitalia or pudenda. Instead, Lucy was said to have 'berated' the Vice-Chancellor 'following her controversial sacking from the university's deeply troubled Creative Writing Department'. She had obviously refused to speak to Heston, and there were no quotations from her. Amy Burdage-Pask said there had been a 'misunderstanding' at the *College Collage* party, 'swiftly rectified, however'. Ballaugh's office gave an anodyne statement in which the Vice-Chancellor expressed his delight that *College Collage* had reached its tenth anniversary and looked forward confidently 'to many more successful decades because of the high quality year-in-year-out of undergraduate journalism'.

A couple of London papers picked up the story and published light-hearted accounts of the birthday turmoil, mostly on their special Education page, though without citing what Lucy had said, either printed full out or coded. 'Fired Poet Blasts Back' was one banner. A tabloid ran a full-length feature prompted by these reports, asking in its headline, 'So What The Dickens (And Shakespeare And Milton) IS Creative Writing?' There were pictures of these three authors and of Fielding, Hardy, Joyce, Shelley, Steinbeck and Tolstoy. The article asked:

Did any of these famed writers go to creative writing classes to learn how to do it? Why do our universities bother with this makeweight, hogwash subject? Shouldn't our students be learning how to make a living, not playing about pretending to be literary greats, but with no hope of ever reaching that standard? Oh dear, oh dear, a would-be poet gets her marching orders. ho cares? Might it discourage her from scribbling and encourage her to take a real job?

It was on the day after this article appeared that Lucy's poems made the *Times Literary Supplement*.

Eight

In a way, the sudden lift in Lucy's rating pleased Len Maldave. Previously, there had been that blatant difference of literary grade between himself as an established writer, and her as novice and acolyte. Frankly, she was nowhere. This gulf looked so great to him that he'd decided it would be wrong to make any kind of sexual drive for Lucy, despite the tidy way her jeans fitted; improper to use his undoubted status in an attempt to pull her. Such an approach could have amounted to what the reporter called *droit de seigneur*, that monstrous right of a feudal lord to have any local girl first. He must not take advantage of Lucy's unavoidable admiration for his status and his work. But, post-*TLS,* he thought that when she returned with whatever amendments and additions she had for *In Times Of Broken Light* he would feel much more at ease with her, because now he could discard his worries about being so blazingly, embarrassingly superior.

He had not seen Lucy since she went off with his novel, promising to work on it. Her personal email address still figured in the departmental directory although she'd been sacked, and he naturally sent her congratulations on the *TLS* poems, yet with no badgering queries about the script. She'd be elated and preoccupied by the *Supplement* spread. He must show patience. Lucy had earned this. Maldave considered it might not be stupid exaggeration even to say she had reached a kind of creative equality with him via this one issue of the *Supplement*. It meant he could regard her as a woman, not as a vulnerable votary intent on pleasing him. He hated any *de haut en bas* relationship: that type of patronizing connection between someone supposedly well-placed and someone lowly; hated it if he was supposedly the *de haut*, never mind how much he might actually *be* the *de haut*, as, in this case, he clearly had been via his several accomplishments, pre Lucy's poems and leg up.

But then Maldave began to wonder whether Lucy would, in fact, continue her interest in his typescript now she had triumphed so splendidly. Suddenly, on publication day of that *TLS* issue, she'd moved into a different category. Fame, prestige – they were unquestionably hers. Good God, perhaps *she'd* become the fucking *de haut,* and he the *en bas* bit. Would Lucy glance at the file cover of his script and ask herself, 'Do I need bother with this ruin?' After all, she knew about *In Times Of Broken Light*'s rejections saga. Lucy would probably want to capitalize on her *gloire* and write new material of her own while her name was hot, not fiddle with trying to resuscitate his. He hoped he could understand this. Egomania: not admirable but regrettably commonplace among writers.

Maldave himself had had publication days, of course – *Placards, Nursery*; some poems and 'See Overleaf' in *College Collage*; and other poems in a mid-West, US university magazine. But *his* publication days never got distinguished from any other day. Hardly a soul seemed to know they *were* his publication days. It was like screaming to the world from a closed, sound-proofed room. He remembered waking up on the morning *Scimitar* came out and murmuring excitedly to Elaine – she was still around then – 'Publication day, Elly. *Nursery Scimitar.*'

'*Nursery* fucking WHAT?'

'Well, *Scimitar.*'

'Honestly?'

'A sort of oxymoron: contrast of the homely harmlessness of a child's room against the potential violence of a sword, an exotic sword, scimitar being oriental.'

'Yea?' she replied, about to get back fast to unconsciousness. 'So the day's special? Who for? I need to notice?' Harsh. Fair. That's how Elly always was. She felt left out of his literary triumphs and therefore resented and/or ignored them. He gathered Elly had moved on to an ice hockey star now. He might be able to freeze some respect into her.

No launch parties billed to Len's publisher took place at the Groucho Club or the Savoy in London for *Placards* or *Nursery*. No, no placards for *Placards*. Review pages in the heavy papers did not rush to notice him; in fact, they rarely noticed him at all, early or late or Among The Rest. Things would not be like this for Lucy. Impact. That's what quantity exposure in the *TLS* gave. He wondered if Lucy sent in a photograph of herself with her work – possibly full length – perhaps more than one. Obviously, the *TLS* did not publish that kind of picture, but a portrait of her – possibly full length – might have ... well, *impact* with an editor. Maldave considered any photograph of Lucy would convince those looking at it she smelled grand, even without scent: just her flesh, in every area, most likely.

156

He did not mean the poems had no merit if judged apart from Lucy's appearance. Of course they did. Of course. However, the thing was, it would be no use Maldave relying on *his* face or body to give work that additional push. He had to make *his* impact through, for example, titles of extra gleam and grab quality – such as *Placards on High, Nursery Scimitar* and *In Times Of Broken Light*. Vanessa Dale, in the C.W. class, as well as Lucy herself, had mentioned the enticing power of *In Times Of Broken Light*, as a name for a novel, despite his difficulties so far in getting the book taken. Incidentally, it was Vanessa who produced the quip, 'No placards for *Placards*,' apparently intended as sympathy, the fucking back row joker. Although Maldave liked wit, there should be limits.

It had really cheered him when Lucy came to his flat following that *College Collage* imbroglio. This gladness in Maldave was extremely specific to Lucy, not a matter for all womankind. Although he'd never really missed having a partner at home with him since Elaine went, it thrilled him to look at Lucy seated opposite in the living room. Her visit lasted less than a couple of hours, yet when she left he felt desolate. Deprivation moved in, and he longed for her return.

Somehow, she seemed to complete the room. Len had always liked this part of the flat, even when alone there – or even *especially* when alone there – after the sad, recurring unpleasantnesses with Elaine. Yet now the absence of Lucy definitely struck him as a lasting loss. He missed that special smell of her, a kind of soothing, lemonadey smell.

For a while, yes, he had resented how she tried to take over *In Times Of Broken Light*, so damned blithely and fast, especially as this happened, of course, on that day when, for a while, she seemed distressed and in need of solace, after the party disturbance. He'd felt confused by the turn-around. Suddenly, *she* was looking after *him*, and what she called his 'failed' script. This wounded. Len did not mind accuracy in conversation or writing. In fact, he strove for it personally and loathed roundabout language and euphemisms. Didn't he admire Swift's and Orwell's prose for its grand, no-nonsense quality? Just the same, 'failed' seemed insolently cruel, coming from a bloody kicked-out kid beginner in the creativity game, however nicely assembled. This had been pre-*TLS* triumph, of course. She remained just Lucy then. Couldn't she have said 'challenging script', or 'bracingly-non-populist script'?

Later, though, he decided her instincts to

158

help him had been genuine and without condescension. He saw, too, that, for someone of her approaching literary distinction, to bother helping on a re-write of work with such a null record revealed extraordinary kindness. Now, the *TLS* acceptances gleamed, and she might be gone for keeps. God, he wished she would come back, bringing more ideas for *Broken Light,* sexing up ideas if she wished, but, in any case, come back ... Lucy – seven-string-prodigy, beauty, cunt-caller, come back.

He went in to take a Creative Writing workshop and try to forget about her for a while, in case he needed to forget about her altogether. She might never reappear with his script. That would not be fatal from a publishing point of view: he had *Broken Light* on disk, of course. But forget Lucy? He soon came to realize how simple-minded that was: of course the students knew about the *TLS*, and Lucy's glory, and wanted to discuss this and not much else. Just the same, Maldave tried to get them on to a safer subject, on to more localized, less public, creativity. And, for a while, it worked. In pursuit of the reasonably normal, Maldave had Dave Merry read a poem he'd written called 'Nature'. It figured a tree outside his house whose leaves collected soot and grime in the atmosphere from nearby factories and, when the weight of filth reached critical point, tipped the whole lot into the street, like coal or coke down a freighter chute. Then the leaves would right themselves and start dirt collecting once more. Merry did not often contribute writing, seemed half knocked-off for much of the time by what Len guessed to be the other kind of coke. Today, though, his designated nostril looked less vermilion and tattered, his eyes in touch with things around. Maldave felt obliged to give him and his poem special encouragement. Incidentally, there had been a rumour a while back that he and A. F. W. Ichbald were lovingly shacked up and snort-sharing. Len wondered what effect the sackings might have had for them.

As to Dave's 'Nature', Maldave said he admired the way an apparently Romantic Movement title, indeed, a *Wordsworthian* title, was 'qualified and undercut' by the actual urban-drab contents of the poem. He praised Dave's use of mathematical and scientific factors, like the so-called metaphysical poets of the seventeenth century.

'Me?' Dave replied.

'Oh, yes, absolutely.' Maldave added that the poem managed to mix learning and passion – passionate rage in this case – *so* brilliantly. He suggested the key verse came after a close description of how the airborne pollution reaches and piles up on the tree until, scientifically:

> Strictly in accord with Newton's
> fucking law, this granulated
> muck then seeks a downward route
> towards the centre of the earth,
> but finds my Citroen's once-white roof
> and makes a filthy stop.

Vanessa found *'once-white'* and *'and makes a filthy stop'* extremely notable. *'Once-white'* told us of the constant messing up of the car and symbolized the increasing grubbiness of life itself. She also explained that the short line *'and makes a filthy stop'* worked brilliant-ly 'because, like, it *stops* the verse, just as the car roof stops the tumbling, staining dirt. The poem, like, *performs* what it's describ-ing.'

'Enacts,' Maldave said. 'Exactly, I—'

'What about the Lucy Corth Show, though, Len?' Vanessa replied. 'That *TLS* take-over by her. Seven poems. I mean, seven! A seven-branch candelabra of bright achievement.'

'Candelabrum,' Maldave replied. 'Singular.'

'Oh, this is much, much more than singular!' Vanessa cried. 'Phenomenal.'

'I meant candelabra was the plural form, but you're talking about only one candelabrum. Latin. Yes, Lucy's success is clearly very interesting.'

'Oh, interesting! Come on. A bit more than that, don't you think?' Vanessa said. 'This is what I mentioned the other day about the battling here, and the way it, like, disrupts us, maybe blights us.'

'"Us"? Which us?' Maldave asked.

'Us, the students,' she replied.

'Disrupts?' Maldave said. 'Blights? Aren't you rather over-the-top, Van?'

'Am I? Lucy, a great and recognized poet who used to tutor, is now gone,' Vanessa said. 'A *published* poet. Big published, not some rag. But she's unavailable to us – that's us, the students, still – she's unavailable to us, the students, any longer. Why? Where's the sense?'

Yes, in God's name, where? Might there in fact be *no* sense, only sickening, modish political dogma – and blatant error? Maldave disliked the hint that the tutors who remained, such as himself, could not rate with Lucy Corth.

'Everyone's heard she called the Vice-Chancellor a cunt,' Dave Merry said. 'Is this what would be termed "poetic licence"? And then in the Press, although cleaned up a bit.'

'Within a university there will always be vigorous debate,' Maldave replied. 'A sign of integrity of views and seriousness. Occasionally language may become colourful.'

'And I suppose as boss of bosses he does look like a right cunt now,' Vanessa said.

'I hate hearing that word as a term of contempt,' Maldave replied. 'So demeaning to women.'

'Looks like a prick, then,' Vanessa said. 'What's the difference? I mean, as epithet, obviously. Neither's a bouquet. Listen, Len, we're taking on a lifetime's debt to pay fees here and are entitled to the best staff. Yet Lucy gets the arbitrary heave-ho. We might have a real grievance. In law, I mean.' She grew suddenly milder: 'And listen, listen, Len, are *you* safe? I mean *you*, in person.'

'Safe?'

'Yes, safe,' Vanessa replied.

'Why not?' he said.

She thought about this for a second. Then, when Vanessa spoke again, her voice slipped further into gentleness, became even tentative, certainly not suited to shouting orders above the noise of a desert tanks conflict.

'Look, Len,' she said, 'are you like shagging Lucy Corth? Poetic licentiousness.' Immediately, she held up one hand as apology, as pretended disclaimer of what she'd just said 'A bit personal, maybe, but we felt we had to ask. The class saw this as an obviously very delicate matter and wanted someone with tact to float the question, so elected yours truly. I ask again: are you shagging Lucy? As is famous now, you did a real considerate look-after on her following the *College Collage* spat. Was this a convenient way of getting started with her?'

'Lucy is a friend,' Maldave said.

'Yea, but like I mean something *going* with her?' Vanessa replied. 'She's a peach and talented. It would be understandable. Possibly deep – not just gratification. This could be perilous for you, couldn't it, Len? We worry. Ballaugh chucks her as part of a vicious, money-raising ambition, so what's likely to happen to someone like you if you're snuggling up there, Len?'

Cuddling up, the reporter had said. Now, Van with *snuggling* up. He wished.

'Ballaugh ... well, he can be tough, that's clear. Economist. Into figures and balance sheets,' Vanessa said. 'Will he see you as treacherous and despicable and dangerous? The risk could be greater now Lucy's championed by the *TLS*. It's the sort of thing that will make Ballaugh look stupid, won't it? It *has* made him look stupid. Well, he might panic and turn on anyone associated with Lucy, as Macbeth goes berserk when menaced and kills nearly everyone around. Or Adolf after one of the plots. So, you, too, get dismissed? This department would disintegrate without Len Maldave. We'd be lost, Len. An irreplaceable bond.'

'The dismissal was a policy matter, limited, complete,' Maldave replied. 'Don't forget A. F. W. Ichbald went as well.'

'Who says complete?' Vanessa replied. 'It like stinks.'

Huw Gance, lolling in the second row, had seemed uninterested in the conversation. He wore a pale blue, black buttoned, very clean, open-necked shirt, the kind of thing authors performing as critics on TV's *Newsnight Review* might pick, trying hopelessly, fatuously, to prove unpretentiousness. Now, though, he said: 'Could you get shown the door next, Len? That's bad. Oh, all right, we do a bit of joshing and teasing, but we know you hold this department together, and that, without you, it's finished. You bring experience. The world recognizes you and your work.' Of course, Maldave listened, and listened, for the under-burble of sarcasm and contempt

165

in Gance's voice. And, to his astonishment, failed to detect them. Perhaps Huw could do sincerity now and then, the duplicitous sod.

'The possibility of losing you *really* makes us anxious, Len,' Vanessa said.

'Too true,' Dave Merry said.

'My God, it would be awful,' Daisy Nelmes said, a tall, thin, close-cropped blonde poet who showed up at the classes around one in four or five, and had written vivid verses as by an oldie about the diciness of walking on pavemented wet leaves. 'We need you, Dr Maldave.' She was not present often enough to progress to his first name. He loathed being called Dr. Generally, writers didn't have titles. All right, it had been *Dr* Johnson – a rare exception. Doctorates showed you could read up stuff well. Only that. Passive. It was *teachers* who sported their Ph.Ds. He was very much more than a teacher and so wanted to be addressed as less.

Suddenly, all four of those who had spoken this afternoon – Vanessa, Dave Merry, Huw Gance and Daisy Nelmes – left their places and came unhurriedly, gravely, to the front of the room just in front of Len's table-desk. It had to be a rehearsed move. But meaning what? Daisy stood very still, very tall and tree-like, staring nowhere, the way a tree might on a still day. Dave took a position in front of Daisy, facing away, his back pressed against her. He had his arms behind him, one on each side of Daisy. Gance and Vanessa went to the far side of the room and raised *their* arms up to near their faces, left out furthest, the right bent to just under their noses, as if they held rifles and were aiming.

Almost together, they each made the sound of a shot with their lips. Dave Merry slowly went to the ground at Daisy's feet. She stayed motionless. Vanessa walked forward and now, as with a pistol, not a rifle, pointed a couple of fingers down at Dave's head and mimicked the explosion of another shot. After that, the three of them, Gance, Vanessa and Daisy, gathered around Dave where he lay on the floor and flung their hands and arms high and to the sides and occasionally tugged at their hair, though it was hard for Daisy to get a grip. Dave stood eventually, the four bowed to Len, and they trooped back to their places.

As the performance ended, Maldave realized he had witnessed a little exercise in *avant garde* mime drama. Of course, that was wholly valid in a Creative Writing class. He thought he could interpret it. The playlet showed, of course, an execution by firing squad, complete with *coup de grâce* from

Vanessa's pistol. Daisy was the wooden post against which Dave, as victim, had been notionally tied, his arms behind him. A sort of post-modern post. No wonder she had that tree look. Maybe she always had a bit of a tree look – a conifer – but she managed extra for the sketch, a kind of wholehearted, sappy, Method embodiment of treeness.

And then, near the end, as in the style of certain contemporary theatre, Daisy, Gance and Vanessa shed their original roles and became mourners over dead Dave, performing classical or Mid-East wave-it-about grief gestures and hair-tearing. Naturally, Maldave realized he was the victim, topped for traitorous association with Lucy Corth. Gance and Vanessa represented the university, or the system, or the C. W. department, or the Minister or all Ministers, Vanessa starring as executioner with the dispatch shot. They intended a warning. Their parable said, *They're ganging up on you, Leonard.* It was kind – yes, almost certainly it was kind. Hadn't Gance asked if Len might get axed? In their one-act drama, he didn't get axed, he got the bullet. Perhaps they exaggerated the hazards in his situation. After all, he had a staff job, with a lifelong contract, not like Lucy on trial, her agreement with the university renewable, or not, yearly. But, of course, universities did find ways of kicking out even supposedly permanent lecturers if someone powerful took a hate to them. Ballaugh remained powerful. He had the Government behind him, pushing him to ruthlessness.

Maldave did not tell the class his own position was passably secure and that, on the face of it, anyway, he could not get fired for anything short of turpitude with bells on, openings for which never arrived. To disclose this would have spoiled their grand, astonishing display of affection and dependence – even that sod, Gance. Schmaltz had a valid place in life's scheme, particularly when the scheme was creativity. Ambiguity also had a valid place in life's scheme, particularly when the scheme was creativity: did this quartet, and perhaps the rest, mean what had been said about him and his teaching role just now? Was he truly treasured? They lived in terror of losing him, because Creative Writing would irreparably splinter without Maldave? Or had they laid on a pre-arranged piss-take? 'Like, how about we give Leonard – acclaimed author of *Placards On High* and *Nursery Scimitar* – some hogwash?' Vanessa might have asked the others. 'Let's stick him in a drama, right? Yes, stick him.'

Now, though, she said: 'We must force

them to bring Lucy back. If she'll come. Perhaps she's moved too far above this place. Perhaps she feels so resentful and insulted by her sacking she'd tell them they can stuff the job.'

God, she might. Maldave said: 'Can we please return to Dave's work about casual victimization of the ordinary man and his car by corporate industry?'

'Is that what it says, Len?' Dave Merry asked.

Maldave said: 'What I also like here is the suggestion in the opening stanza that it is not just the car owner, ie, obviously Mankind, who is affected by the factory discharge, but nature itself, in the image of the tree, has also been made sick, like the rose in William Blake's poem. Poignant. Cosmic.' Maldave read Dave's first stanza aloud. It might be a way of keeping them off the Lucy topic.

Ecologically this tree
is into a bad time and once
or twice – no, more than that – I've thought
I'll cut the gawky fucker down:
an axe and chain-saw job, to save
it from itself.

'So moving,' Maldave said. 'So fresh and apt.'

'Yes, cutting things down,' Vanessa said. 'To the nasty point? Overtones? Accidental topicality? A while ago, we had that Minister around, Mr "Call me Mo", you know, Len, accompanied by his Vice-Chancellorship, the Principal, hobnobbing together in the Common Room, talking to undergraduates, glasses of Fanta, smiles and accessibility, doing the democratic.'

'Yes, I remember,' Maldave said.

'Mo's got an education but like he's turned against it,' Vanessa replied. 'For now. I asked them about Lucy – why we'd lost her – why she'd been cut down. This was before the *TLS*. I just wanted to know where all the aggro in the university – in universities – came from, and whether, please God, it would end soon. But no real answers. I've realized since – it's all political, isn't it? Mo said "reorganization", "a radical re-think on Creative Writing nationwide", but then it was wool and more wool. No good saying to him that Lucy, and others, such, of course, as yourself, Len, had been teaching us brilliantly how to write well. As far as I could see, Mo thinks any piece of writing is as good as any other, as long as it comes from "people". Well, I said I never heard of a moth writing – I told you, I'm the one with tact. I asked him, does the *New Yorker* think any piece of writing as good as any other? Try getting a piece in there, Minister, I said.'

Dave Merry, who occasionally seemed to suffer from a bad dose of literary theory as well as various powders said: 'But there could be debate over the meaning of "good" in this context.'

'"Good" means it works,' Vanessa replied.

'The print on a cornflakes packet "works",' Dave said. 'It tells you about the cornflakes.'

'So, Mo has a cornflakes packet on his bedside table in case of sleeplessness?' Vanessa said.

Daisy said: 'Remember those lines near the start of *The Waste Land*? "In the mountains, there you feel free. I read Kellogs blurbs most nights, and go south in the winter."'

'Like I considered asking Mo, "OK, if there's no good or bad writing, only writing, why have classes in it, Outreach or here? Why classes at all, ever?"' Vanessa said. 'But then big, big panic. I realized the half-baked bugger might get convinced by that argument and decide to shut the department down completely, instead of just fucking it about, so I didn't.'

'They'll want Lucy back,' Daisy said, 'Ballaugh and the Senate – all of them. I mean, taking into account the *TLS*.'

'It's uncertain,' Dave Merry replied.

'Totally,' Vanessa said.

'If you're actually sleeping with her, Dr Maldave, they might see you as a useful go-between,' Daisy said. 'Someone to carry apologies and a plea for forgiveness. But it wouldn't be just a matter of, pardon the term, your sexual familiarity. You're very much someone with a literary status in your own right – *Placards On High*, *Nursery Scimitar*, plus poems and the ECOC membership – and they'd prize you as able to talk to her entirely on a par, literary figure to literary figure, even with her new distinction. At least that.'

Maldave detested the phrase 'in your own right'. It made him or anyone else sound like a forever also-ran. Profiles in the Press might say: 'The Field Marshal's wife is distinguished in her own right – she personally shampoos the labradors at their lovely Hampshire home.' He wasn't a fucking writer in his own right, he was a fucking writer, *tout court*, as Dape might say.

'Ballaugh will want her back now, it's true.' Vanessa said. 'But Mo? He's supremo – supreme-Mo – and Mo doesn't believe in status. Not *literary* status – not yours, Len, not Lucy's, not Rudyard Kipling's. Naturally, he believes in his own – as supremo – and draws the pay and allowances. But writers? Anyone will do, as long as they're *people*. I could see he's worked it out like one of those old time logic arguments, with two statements and then a pay-off.'

'Classical syllogism,' Gance said.

Vanessa said: 'Goes like this: first premise: *Writers are people*. Second premise: *We're all people*. Conclusion: *We're all writers*. Or another version: first premise: *Writers express themselves*. Second premise: *We all express ourselves*. Conclusion: *As above*. Worth doesn't get a look in. The Man Booker competition for best novel every year? Silly subjectivity, with a pot of money on the end. Nobel Prize for Literature? More so, both. F. R. Leavis's "Great Tradition" of novels? Élitist academic horseshit. Remember when Napoleon said after the Revolution and *liberté, fraternité, égalité*, "We must have distinctions"? The Minister would regard that as thundering heresy. And so to Lucy's *TLS* poems. For Minister Mo they're just printed poems, the same as those tortured death notice jingles in the local weekly:

You left us ere the morning light
had brought a new bright day.

174

Yours had been a brave, long fight,
but now you've gone away.

Mo would say there's as much true feeling in
that as in any other piece of verse – Lucy's,
Shelley's, Verlaine's. OK, so, *Paradise Lost* is
longer. But Milton didn't have to pay small
ad rates for it.'

'We could go on strike,' Dave Merry said.

'Who?' Maldave replied.

'The students,' Merry said. 'Pickets. Ban-
ners – "Reinstate Lucy Corth and A. F. W.
now!" "No Victimization of Len Maldave."'

'Are you still living with A. F. W., Dave?'
Maldave asked. 'People would think this the
only reason for your protest.'

'We'd be on our own,' Vanessa said. 'Other
students wouldn't come out for sacked C. W.
staff.'

'All right, just us,' Daisy said. 'It might
make the media. Ballaugh won't want that.
Not good for his sacred mission.'

'Which?' Vanessa said.

'To make the university look good. And
stop it going broke,' Daisy said.

Nine

A Mo phone call bringing what at first sight seemed happy news really shook Ballaugh. Things changed damn fast. Or, at least, Mo-type things did. Ballaugh wasn't sure he could keep up.

Naturally, even before this, he'd begun to wonder whether his job was too big for him. There'd been that joke of Fiona's claiming he had shrunk so much lately – shrunk in actual stature – yes, shrunk so much Fiona felt relief if she could spot Caspar around the house, presumably so there'd be no danger of vacuuming him into the dust bag. Fiona did like merrymaking. Probably kindness prompted her in this instance. Maybe she worried about his declining condition, as she saw it, but would never express head-on concern. She'd think that alarmist or senti-mental. Fiona had real feelings for him, no question, surely. Apparently, though, when she was a child, her father would persist in attempts to be witty, and perhaps this made her think humour had a due place in the home, like bleach or a sideboard. Ballaugh recalled that line in one of Lucy Corth's poems about a joke being forced to do a fair day's work, like waitresses or trawlermen.

Just the same, did Fiona's damn quip about him reach an awkward truth, as quips occasionally did? He found his mind shoved back to something he'd read a good time ago about people successful in their careers until ... until ... When first he considered aiming for a Vice-Chancellorship, he'd decided he had better mug up some higher executive skills: after all, a Vice-Chancellor ran not just a department of a university, but a university, and at that time Ballaugh lacked top leadership form. Wasn't there a case somewhere of an ex-professor of chemistry returning from Africa to take a Vice-Chancellorship and by ineptness in this larger job destroying the university college he ran – tried to run?

So, Ballaugh consulted a few books on business and boardroom practice. And, in one of these, he came across the frightening, depressing theory that go-ahead people got promoted and promoted and promoted until they reached one step beyond their competence; one doomed, disastrous, final step. It was an oldish book, by an author he thought surnamed Peters or Peter. Did this law still apply? Could tearaway whiz-kids suddenly become star flops and the trauma make their frame dwindle? Ballaugh wondered whether another reasonably capable professor – of Economics and Business, not chemistry – ie, himself – might turn into a catastrophic Vice-Chancellor. Or possibly into a cunt. Perhaps had *already* turned into a cunt. He doubted his management skills. As it happened, few of these had been used in the treatment of Corth and A. F. W. Ichbald. Simply, they had to be pushed aside in the quickest way available so that money-making could be accelerated in other departments: irresistible Government thinking. *I vos only obeying orders.*

Subsequently, Ballaugh seemed to become half swamped in an uncomfortable mix of literature – or, at least Creative Writing – and politics. Other departments had suffered his axe, but it was Creative Writing that gave the true, persistent aggro. He found it tough to make sense of either of these – C.W. and politics – but especially when they overlapped: that is, tough to make his kind of precise, definable, constant sense.

This bloody morning, for instance, when the phone rang he found himself caught up in both of them. Plus, of course, on the literary side, he already had spiky recollections of Fiona's Outreach verse demo the other night. That really brought him tremors. If she wanted to go poetic in public he wished she could have chosen a safer topic, like the elderly writer's about rabbit slaughter in the 1940s. Fiona was too young for that, obviously, but there must be other similarly non-sexual areas, such as those items often found in poetry like flowers or meadows or the environment generally. The uncuff-linked, hatless man waiting for her in the poem bothered him. Ballaugh would not usually have had views about cuff-links either way, but the poem hinted that their probable absence on those wrists indicated someone shady, even louche, although he'd turned up early for the date. Would you want your wife experiencing experience between spruced up but experienced sheets with someone experienced like that, or even want her fantasizing about the experience, if the poem were just a bit of an unspruce dream and not actual experience?

Mo came through on his private, non-switchboarded line in the office. Yes, he spoke politics. Yes, he spoke literature. Mo knew how to overarch. One day he might be not just a Minister but a Cabinet Minister. It seemed inappropriate for a politician with so much head and authentically appalling lineage to be in only a middle-ranking post, especially when you thought of some of the people who were already in the Cabinet. 'Casp, lad, I report developments.'

'Yes?'

'Good developments. In fact, unquestionably brilliant developments.'

Ballaugh felt uncertain what 'good' meant in Mo's grading of matters. On the whole, though, he thought that Mo's 'good' might not inevitably strike him, Ballaugh, as totally and irrecoverably fucking bad. 'This sounds promising, Mo,' he said. But Ballaugh feared the 'in fact' and the 'unquestionably'. If such things had to be said, it generally meant the opposite.

'Here it is, then, Casp, we get a whisper now, and a strong one, even an indisputable one, that your noble city will make it to a short list of three for the Culture title.'

'Grand, Mo.'

'The other two on the list, foreign: Palermo in Sicily and Dresden, Germany. It's undoubtedly progress.'

'Splendid.'

'Fine for the city, fine for the university – supposing the short list is only the beginning.'

'Great.'

'This might entail some adjustments, clearly.'

'Adjustments?' No, not clearly at all. Not to Ballaugh.

'Very fine fine-tuning, in certain respects, Casp.'

Which, you froth-mouthed bastard? 'I know the Committee here have been really working at the City Of Culture campaign. Fruitful sessions. Many. One of our lecturers is a member. They, indeed, deserve success.'

'Indeed. Indeed. There's acute Cabinet interest.'

'Grand.'

'Culture's what we refer to at Westminster as a "priority growth theme", Casp.'

'Who?'

'In Government thinking,' Mo replied. 'Culture comes up as a topic more than you'd expect, despite Iraq, ID cards, bombs, and pensions and the NHS.'

' "Priority growth theme" is a catchy phrase.'

'You've not come across it before? You'll ask, in your inquiring, economist-trained way for a definition.'

'It's obviously a positive,' Ballaugh said. No, not at all so damn obviously.

'I think I can put this plainly – escape from jargon. A priority growth theme occurs in

181

some sector of policy where advance is seen as vital from the point of view of benefit to the country and, therefore, popular approval.'

'Electoral?'

'What?'

'Popular approval,' Ballaugh replied. 'You mean the theme brings in votes?'

'The PM himself is extremely focused on culture. And the Deputy means to get much closer to it any day now. He's got to fit culture in with quite a whack of other stuff, though. He naturally has his own priority growth schemes.'

'Of course, Mo.'

'But, for instance, Casp, the Deputy would never use that allegedly Goering quote, "When I hear anyone talk of culture I reach for my revolver."'

'Culture is—'

'The PM is determined to improve the profile of GB. The culture profile of GB.'

'A magnificent aim.'

'He's very conscious of the GB heritage and feels more could be made of it. He wants culture projected. There's Purcell – a talented composer. Is enough made of him? Then *The Merry Wives Of Windsor*, and other works of that type. Or Graham Sutherland and the way he did many a genuine cliff and its strata. We often talk. That's the PM and myself, not Sutherland and I. He's dead. As the PM sees it, culture is as natural to GB as, say, coal used to be. It just needs bringing to the surface, again the same as coal.'

'It's heartening that the PM should be—'

'I don't mean revival of that fucking crass and sprawling "Cool Britannia" programme. Very much the day before yesterday's concept, and not much of a one then. But culture as true culture, in the widest sense. This is not to exclude *multi*culture. Of course not. Of course not. There's African music, no denying. But also we must put justified emphasis on home-grown Brit-as-Brit culture. The eclectic. Music, sculpture, paint, writing – you name it. Of and for the people. A broad brush. That's not just in the visual arts aspect. A broad brush generally. All-encompassing.'

'Right.'

'Neither the PM, nor myself, would be happy about a culture that did not include the people as integral.'

'I would have guessed that.'

'I mean, if we consider culture on its own – admirable in some ways, no doubt – but what is it without people?' Mo said. 'The people and culture should go hand-in-hand.'

'This can't be gainsaid.'

183

'If you take something like Graham Sutherland and the cliffs, their strata, these are items that can be seen by everyone. A seaside visit and there's a good chance there'll be cliffs, with strata. Then, when people encounter a Graham Sutherland painting of these cliffs with strata it will be plain what he's getting at. This is not some chi-chi, hidden-away topic. People will have witnessed these cliffs for themselves on holiday or a day-trip. They can and will relate. The PM and I have complete trust in the people – their ability to react to cliffs and strata when painted and so on. These cliffs are an open door to culture. This is our objective.'

'He's the one who did Churchill, isn't he?'

'Who?'

'Sutherland.'

'Cliffs are his main thing. He could make strata tell a story. There was a museum with his stuff down in West Wales.'

'Churchill's wife hated the picture, destroyed it.'

'If someone's main thing is cliffs and strata they're not going to be used to somebody like Churchill.'

'She thought it made him look like a toad.'

'Who?'

'Churchill's wife.'

'This is the point about artists – they paint

what they see. So, strata. This brings me to my news, Casp.'

'Oh, I thought the shortlisting was that.'

'As I and the PM regard it, Casp, your city encapsulates, symbolizes, in this competition, the whole GB cultural identity. You are, as it were, our chosen champion.'

'If we win.'

'Exactly. What I wanted to speak about,' Mo replied. Ballaugh sensed that some difficult, possibly confusing, complexity was about to bubble from Mo. 'Adjustments.' The voice of the Minister who disliked being called Minister had turned ministerial for repetition of this word. That is, commanding, full of party-squawk, super-bullshitty instead of standard-bullshitty, evasive, unapologetic, in touch with meaning, but not slavishly in touch. He would perhaps be speaking less his own thoughts than those of the focused Prime Minister and the focused Cabinet. He was mouthpiecing the message. 'We *must* win this one, Casp.'

'Well, absolutely, Mo, and I'm sure the City of Culture Committee here will do all—'

'When I say fucking Dresden, they'll have a damn sympathy thing going for them. You see that, do you?'

'Sympathy?'

185

'On account of that air raid business in the war, you know. It's quite famous and therefore a reckonable element when we come to a competition of this kind.'

'You mean the wipe-out of the city by Allied inferno fire bombing in 1945?'

'Context, Casp. We must look at that in context. Regrettable, of course, of course. Controversial, certainly. Didn't our ambassador over there say sorry for it lately? And then the Queen herself went to Dresden. This is sure to encourage the kraut bastards. It's sixty fucking years ago, yet still a fucking factor, because the Dresden people will *make* it a fucking factor in some subtle, damned unpredictable ways. We've got to counter that.'

'How would we...?'

'And then, what to say about Palermo? Mafia land. *They* don't give a toss about culture, but they'll see the potential for their whores and pushers and casinos if the tourist flow goes up because Palermo wins and the place is full of intellectuals and aesthetes keen to express themselves. So, from Palermo, all kinds of gangster pressures on the City Of Culture judges. Do you see where my mind's going? It's rather suspicious, isn't it, that both the other shortlisted places are in countries we beat in the war? Clearly, I'm not anti-Jerry or anti-Eyetie, but these are people trying to sneak back to prominence decades after they got legitimately squashed. The European Union is a splendid concept, who'd doubt it? All the same, one has to wonder when a shortlist like this emerges.'

'The Committee here has many ideas, I'm sure,' Ballaugh replied. 'And they meet a lot. I know our man, Leonard Maldave, is often over at the Civic Buildings. He's someone with plenty to give the Committee himself. A novelist. Well, I expect you'll have come across his works, Mo – *Nursery Scimitar*, *Placards On High*. Did I mention them before? Impressive volumes, rather than run-of-the-mill best sellers. He'll keep the Committee positive.'

'And we're naturally right behind him and them in their attempts to contribute,' Mo said.

'Who?'

'The Secretary of State would be proud of him, I'm sure of that. The Secretary of State is a fan of literature. In that all-encompassing sense I mentioned. Not just the great Russian books and Zane Grey but amusing, lighter stuff such as Jane Austen, John Dryden, Noel Coward.'

'This is—'

'Casp, I have to tell you there are several

people up here who read the *Times Literary Supplement,* you know, a quite heavy but worthwhile weekly. It's full of reasonable stuff.'

'Which people?'

'This would be people of clout.'

'The Secretary of State?'

'A surprising number of people,' Mo replied. 'Several in the Department of Trade and Industry, for instance. And in Pensions. They love books and reviews of books, although not working on that actual side of things, more to do with hi-tech factories and benefits. In their own time, their minds range and rove, you see.'

'I think it's healthy when politicians and Civil Servants have general interests outside their specific work,' Ballaugh said. 'Gives balance.'

'This girl, Corth,' Mo replied.

'We've spoken about her before,' Ballaugh said. 'I was extremely grateful for your backing on that issue, the necessary termination of contract issue.'

'Well, yes. Casp, these poems of hers in the weekly just mentioned mean things to people.'

'Some people are very keen on poetry, contemporary and other,' Ballaugh replied.

'Well, they are, they are. It's a taste, and

undoubtedly part of the heritage already referred to. It gets to them, Casp. For some, poetry is not just a drag you had to do in school – "The sea, the sea, the open sea, the blue, the fresh, the ever-free." They get into deeper stuff. I don't mean in the sense of deeper than the sea, which would be non-sense. Deeper in an intellectual way. There's many a poem I admire myself. A poem can really hit a tone, reveal true emotion. This would be especially true with the major poets. It can be men or women. Certainly. Sexual equality in that game even at an early date. For instance, there's two Brownings, of course, female and male, and likewise Rossettis. And this is well over a hundred years ago. Terrific, really. The stuff on the page of people like these is multi-layered often, like the Graham Sutherland cliffs. You have to unpick. And then those wattled cotes you pointed out in the picture at your house that ended up in a poem. They have a continuing significance. Bound to.'

'A good reminder of our rural heritage, Mo, despite industrialization. Perhaps you or I might have been untying wattled cotes even now if things hadn't gone the way they did in history.' Ballaugh talked and gibbered so as to fend off. He feared something tricky and shifty and unscrupulous would come from the Minister soon. He *knew* something tricky and shifty and unscrupulous would come from the Minister soon. He was a Minister, wasn't he? And always, Ballaugh stayed aware that Mo was not just a Minister himself but the son of a Minister, and a Minister who made it to the Cabinet. Two-timing would be built in to Mo. With Mo, two-timing must be congenital. You could put one of those mathematical dots against his name, meaning a figure recurred in an answer *ad infinitum* – in his case, two-timing.

Ballaugh tried to keep the prattle going but knew he would have to pause in the search for more idiocies and that Mo would take over again then. Politics inculcated that quickness and the ability to trample forward over another speaker or interviewer, particularly an interviewer, and then trample back again. Ballaugh continued, or would have, 'A writer like the well-known Matthew Arnold can—'

'Not everyone up here understands why that bright cow poet had to be thrown out,' Mo replied.

'Lucy Corth? But I expect you've been explaining – the overseas students imperative.'

'It's in the nature of my kind of job, Casp, that one does listen and, yes, perhaps has to amend one's views on account of new factors.'

'Oh? Amend?'

'Fixed positions may become irrational or inconvenient positions, even harmful positions. You mentioned Winston Churchill. Well, once a Liberal but finally a Tory. Then again, I think of the Empire State Building, made to yield and sway a little in gales, so that the wind force is dissipated enough.'

'Which people don't understand the sackings?'

'They see a kind of ... well, a kind of contradiction, I suppose one could call it. Yes.'

'In what sense, Mo?'

'She's a creative writer, isn't she, making stuff up, her own stuff, not quoted from others? I've got that right?'

'Oh, yes, this is in the nature of Creative Writing. Hence the word, Creative. Obviously, art is creative, too, but art often has something to start from, such as the cliffs for Graham Sutherland, or Churchill. But with Creative Writing they have to start from scratch, just a sheet of empty paper.'

'What some people here can't comprehend is why a brilliant creative writer should have been banished from the department, I mean, Casp, it being a Creative Writing department, and she being a brilliant creative writer. And this at a time when her skill and reputation are vital to help with the City of Culture campaign on which the PM has supreme focus. I've heard this compared to firing a surgeon because too many patients survive his operations, or sacking a centre forward for scoring a tonne of goals. I'm finding it hard to meet that kind of sharp argument. The people making these points are not the kind I can say, "Oh, piss off" to.'

'I'm sorry you should be having trouble,' Ballaugh replied. 'But, as you'll know, Mo, this was part of a reshaping programme for all universities.'

'Absolutely, and I'll admit that it might well have seemed at first sight that I endorsed this on my visit and approved the sackings.'

'Yes, I certainly thought you—'

'I hope I'm not one to wriggle, Casp. Hardly. I know you'll see a distinction between wriggling on the one hand, and, on the other, not clinging stubbornly and stupidly to a view of things simply because one did at some time take such a view of things. My dad told us at home how upset Harold Wilson became when accused of so-called "weasel words" and "craven back-tracking". Harold much preferred the term "pragmatism". Dad thought Wilson could be said to have brought "pragmatism" into the modern political lexicon.'

Ballaugh had heard it described as 'prat-matism' but didn't say so.

'Let us now apply pragmatism to the situation we have to deal with here, Casp. It's true that I and my colleagues in Government favoured previously what could be called the "Outreach" gospel for our universities. That is, we were not so much interested in students striving to excel and leave their contemporaries behind, but we wanted them to act *with* their contemporaries in the pursuit of knowledge – a "people" experience: knowledge, learning, creativity *for* the people, *by* the people.'

'Yes.'

'But then we suddenly come up against the demands of the City of Culture award. This undoubtedly caused our belief in the equality principle some trouble.'

Ballaugh saw that for once in Mo's slippery gob 'undoubtedly' meant undoubtedly.

'The Culture title is something that has to be won, like a test match or boxing bout. We have to beat the other buggers, Casp, the way we beat those Wops and Nazis. In this context, the neoned success of Corth in the *TLS* is important to us. She has excelled, and we need this excellence, this uniqueness of ability. I certainly do not say, "Sod Out-

193

reach." There are those who definitely *would* say, "Sod Outreach" when faced by the present problems. I do not.'

Inconsequentially, Ballaugh found it bizarre for someone with that enormous and solid-looking head to jig about so much in his opinions, or get pushed about so much in his opinions. This head did not seem to be pulling its weight for Mo. It hadn't got him into the Cabinet yet nor given him steadiness. 'Outreach is a wonderful programme,' Ballaugh said.

'Entirely wonderful,' Mo replied.

'At one of the sessions Fiona recited a poem she'd written. That's *personally* written.'

'Did she, now? Now, did she? Well, there you are.'

'It made me anxious.'

'Why?'

'Sexual.'

'They can be like that,' Mo said.

'Who?'

'Women.'

'How?' Ballaugh replied.

'How what?'

'When you say, "They can be like that," what does "like that" mean? *How* are they "like that"?'

'Put a woman into Outreach and she'll,

well ... reach out,' Mo said. 'It's in their natures.'

'Reach out who to?'

'This can be medicinal,' Mo replied. 'For mature married women. It's well recognized.'

'What?'

'Women in Outreach. They've got things to tell. If they can put it into a lyric, and get people to listen when they read the lyric, they feel realized. They imagine they have an identity. It's part of the equality of the sexes I referred to.'

'*Real* things to tell?'

'These literary folk don't go in for that kind of question, Casp – regard it as a distraction.'

'Which?'

'Real, non-real. They maintain that writing is words on a page. This will seem obvious, but there's a whole stack of theory behind it. The words on the page *are* real – in the evident form of ink and paper – but words on a page are only words on a page and *can* only be words on a page. Other discussion is ... is ... well, improper ... is beyond proper parameters.'

'It had graphicness.'

'What?'

'The poem. Fiona's.'

'Poetry can do that,' Mo said. 'I remember *The Charge Of The Light Brigade*, also from school. Graphic in spades. Cannon to the right of them, but also to the left. Research before he wrote.'

'There's a big mirror and a man without cuff-links waiting in front of it.'

'You can see a lot of those about.'

'What?'

'Big mirrors in bars. They seem to give more space. And men without cuff-links, especially if they're wearing sports-type shirts, where cuff-links might seem too formal. Outreach frees up people's ability to observe,' Mo observed.

'Look, a long while ago I read a story about a Colonel who gets knocked all ways when he finds his wife's a poet. This was before the days of Outreach.'

'When we consider this Corth we're bound to see rare, exceptionally valuable ability, Casp,' Mo replied. 'It must have relevance. Must.'

'Fiona's poem—'

'What we've got to plan, Casp, is how to climb over fucking Dresden and the weepy "Diddums-diddums-then" support it's going to corner thanks to Bomber Harris who put the burn-up planes in, and now this scruffy parade of sorry-saying to them.'

'Plus they've got Messien in Dresden.'

'What's that?'

'High grade china – decorative, artistic, collectable. They would rate as cultural, I expect.'

'They'll have the china to cite as well, then. Probably a lot of it got smashed in the raid but, again I say, this is sixty years ago, so why make a palaver now? China can be replaced. For God's sake, we all do that when we have a breakage in the kitchen. Sweep up, buy new, proceed with life. Any other damn plus you know of for Dresden? Don't tell me that fucker Beethoven was born there will you? They'll steal it.'

'The evening paper here, which is *really* helping with the Culture campaign, says a novelist called Henry Fielding in the seventeen hundreds was not actually born locally but might have stayed in the Telk area when a baby, or come there later. They point out that Fielding wrote a novel called *Tom Jones*, which gives an amusing, though clearly accidental, link with modern pop culture and songs like *The Green, Green Grass Of Home*, though it's true that the *Home* for the current Tom Jones is elsewhere. South Wales. This might come into the City of Culture application.'

'And also we need to rout the Palermo

thug element,' Mo replied. 'Obviously, we – you, your city and university, Casp – can't compete as to the fire blitz point with Dresden because, indisputably, the equivalent never happened in your locality. We'd have heard of it. And I don't suppose the *Scimitar* and *Placards* lad is likely to start terrorizing the City of Culture judges, committed and bright as I'm sure he may be in his own way, but an authorial rather than Sicilian mobster way, like those Palermo sods might. When the PM is focused, as he is on this City Of Culture matter, he brings to such a matter a remarkable ... a remarkable, well, *focus*. And yet a focus which, while certainly pointed and concentrated, also allows superb lateral thinking. I'm referring to this Corth. He's very aware of this Corth.'

'Through people at the DTI and Pensions who read journals?'

'This is a girl who, thanks to her Creative Writing post with you, was very much part of the city, and therefore of the city's case for the Culture title – what I was getting at when I said you and your neighbours down there would be our collective competitor, a representative, for the whole of GB. This girl, I'm advised, is true quality, including what's called a villanelle, apparently – a real tyrant of a form to manage – all kinds of jiggery-pokery with the rhyming, but she's hit it OK – and what we need now is such flagrant quality, so that not even the most bent or threatened fucking judge can miss it.'

'Elton Dape said something like this to me.'

'Dape?'

'The city's Chief Executive. In charge of the City Of Culture campaign.'

'Ah. Yes. He's been on the phone to us here,' Mo said. 'We gave him assurances as to the return of Corth.'

'I don't think he should approach you direct like that. He's not running the university.' Ballaugh wondered now and then whether *anyone* was running it, and whether it mattered much. He said: 'I'm afraid Elton Dape doesn't understand Outreach in the least and—'

'No, I can imagine. But we have to concede that Outreach is not about quality, is it, Casp, not quality *per se*? It's about ... well ... about reaching out, expressing for the sake of expressing, as with Fiona. I'm not saying Fiona is sexually hung up and has to versify her way out of that, if she can, with lust lines aimed at this uncuff-linked man. Outreach is for the people, *all* people, which is an entirely beautiful concept, a twenty-first century concept, yet what must be faced is that, on the whole, the people just as people can't help us land this fucking Culture thing, great and virtually unignorable in their way as the people often are. As far as writing notable poetry that would grab City Of Culture judges is concerned, most people – people as people, I mean – have quite a distance to go – no fault of their own, don't get me wrong, it's just how these things work out. Edmund Spenser – someone like that lives on, but it's tricky for people today to slip into that category. Obviously, I don't say anything against Fiona's poem. She could probably cover a theme of that sort – the kind of pent-up, fervid, intimate sort very well.'

'When you say "advised" about Lucy Corth, who advised you? The people at Trade and Industry or Pensions?'

'It would not surprise me if the PM has read several of the Corth poems himself, or at least asked someone to give him a breakdown on them as to message, structure and mode. He loves to be hands-on, whether it's social services, Africa – and especially Africa – he's made Africa his special patch lately – or Iraq or culture. Villanelles would grab him. I hear there's one poem in the *Supplement* about a manual Stop, Go revolving sign at road works, as an image of the human impulse towards order, where otherwise chaos might ensue, and this would really grab him. Roads and infrastructure are a priority with the PM, as well as order.'

'You want me to get Corth back into her job here, do you?' Ballaugh replied.

'We don't underestimate the difficulty, Casp. She plainly hates you and the place or she wouldn't have pulled that blue-grey plastic chair out from a reserve pile against the wall, carried it some distance across the room, forcing her way through a party-going crowd, climbed on to it in an otherwise pleasant celebration of *College Collage*'s birthday and called you at volume a cunt twice. Number Ten's PR people summarized that day's events to me in those words having had inquiries conducted and I'm sure they'd get it right and, equally, that you have the Government's best wishes in handling it. The Cabinet are keen on investigation, despite the Weapons of Mass Destruction slip-up. Clearly, there's some urgency re Corth. It might be she wants to shake you and your place off her shoes, on account of the savage way you treated her, and move elsewhere. Job offers could flow once people see this show in the *Supplement,* a massive byline making her name memorable. You know that sod Mark Eider over in Wales, don't you? If he decides, "Here's someone gifted and with tremendous tits so I'll recruit her," where the fuck are we, Casp? That's just the kind of thinking Eider specializes in. The City Of Culture bid is too far along for us to transfer it to somewhere in Wales, isn't it? The PM is focused on this city and when he's focused he will not waver, or not often.'

'Who told you she's got terrific tits?'

'It might have been Dape. Would he know something like that? Plus, of course, we've done a little asking around. Corth's on a Number Ten list. This implies a thoroughness of approach. It implies focus, Casp. Is it true?'

'What?'

'About the tits.'

'And then there's Ichbald,' Ballaugh replied.

'Well, certainly. That's only justice. We don't want any unfairness. You can offer Ichbald to Mark Eider if he's recruiting Creative Writers. Do you see someone with a name like Ichbald getting work into the *Times Literary Supplement* or impressing the City of Culture judges?'

'A. F. W. does drama, not poetry, I believe.'

'Corth,' Mo replied. 'Get her. Right?'

This conversation made Ballaugh think he dismally lacked all flair for the larger leadership and its politics. Mo was obviously gifted with such flair, perhaps part inherited from his political father. His views could move sleekly about when pressured, a real talent. Yesterday, he'd thought Outreach supreme. Now, he still thought Outreach signified, but the City Of Culture title signified more, and therefore he'd concentrate on the City Of Culture bid, shelve Outreach and mastermind the retrieval of Corth; *demand* the retrieval of Corth. Ballaugh had felt jarred and disintegrating even before the talk with Mo. Now, he moved on to distraughtness.

A strange solution suggested itself to him, squeezed him into compliance. He decided he must try to locate the bar with the big mirror lit from below which figured in Fiona's poem, 'Procedure'. He wanted to sit there with a drink before the bright looking glass. He thought this might help a little with reconstruction – reconstruction of himself, his personality, his morale. It would make him, wouldn't it, worthy of Fiona's interest? He would cease to be some harassed, dull, gruesomely worthy academic. In the evening, he toured the city centre, searching. It was not just that, if he could see his reflection full and clear, he'd know he remained as previously, instead of crushed by the tripe weight of his job. He might *feel* crushed and infinitesimal, but the glass would show this to be absurd and subjective, a rather hysterical reaction to Fiona's drollery about shrinkage.

He sought more than this, though. He wanted to get himself into a situation where he, too, resembled one of those people referred to in 'Procedure': the kind of nighthawk characters from paintings of the American, Edward Hopper. They sat brilliantly mysterious in front of big bar mirrors. They looked as if they had been pummelled and thumb-screwed by life, perhaps even as much as Ballaugh with these sackings and cunt repercussions, the City Of Culture, and Fiona – but it was this very suffering and confusion that seemed to give them their epic glamour, their picturesque, emblematic grandeur: a grandeur the artist had noticed and caught and immortalized, the way Graham Sutherland did cliffs and strata. Ballaugh wanted to achieve this sad glamour and grandeur through *his* suffering and confusion. He longed to get bigger through being squashed. He'd wear no sodding cufflinks when he reconnoitred for, found and finally installed himself at this remedial bar.

Ten

Yes, Ballaugh could see why Mo might do brilliantly at politics, had already begun to do brilliantly. It was not only his ability to tone in with whatever seemed right for now; and with whatever he had been told to tone in with because it seemed right for now. That would be standard behaviour of any member of any party. But he also went straight to someone's weakness and got his reinforced toecap in there deep and fruitful. Only a genius schemer brought up in a *parti-pris* household could have sensed so accurately how much Ballaugh would be upset and panicked by the idea Lucy Corth might take a job with Mark Eider in Wales.

Ballaugh found it saddened him to contemplate the break with her made so absolute and final, as would happen if she went there. It struck him as unsatisfactory, inadequate, to let a girl like Corth finally quit the area while the hatred she plainly felt for him, and his university, torched on. A so-be-it attitude would never satisfy Ballaugh. Although he believed in management skills, he lacked the shell to guard him from guilt if these skills failed; and it sickened him to know he was intelligently loathed. When Ballaugh's mother had time to consider the boy during his childhood she used to refer to him as 'lovable', and he still wanted to be that, felt he'd earned that. Also, of course, it bruised him to think of Eider scoring, perhaps in all senses. He would have what might be a poetic genius on his staff, a genius and a looker, and a genius and a looker who should be Ballaugh's and would still be Ballaugh's but for Mo's and Mo's superiors' carefully contrived strategy for this university, now reversed.

Regrets bombarded Ballaugh. It had come to seem unchivalrous, unmanly, a dereliction, to hand Corth over to people like Mark and the others around him there. Ballaugh realized he would actually feel something like jilted, yes, jilted, although he had certainly never tried an approach, and this restraint had nothing to do with her damn tallness. No, he imposed on himself a certain sexual ban regarding all students *and* staff, full- and part-time, even towards a girl as clearly purpose-built as Corth. If she joined Eider's crew, Ballaugh would feel he had failed with her, failed all round. Dereliction: undoubtedly the word. He'd find it hard to live with that self-judgement. His confidence leaked and then leaked more. He must certainly locate and visit the illuminated bar mirror flaunted in Fiona's poem and convince himself not that he need not suffer, no, not that, never that, but that his sufferings gave him attractive profound mystery, as well as profound misery. Would Edward Hopper have seen him as symbolic sitting there, and worth an angsty, spirit-of-the-age picture? Ballaugh longed to be symbolic in some interesting, battered fashion. He'd had, and was having, the fucking battering, but could he also provide the interesting bit?

He visualized in detail the kind of email he might get from Eider if he snared Lucy for his operation over there, and for whatever else. Although Ballaugh might be an economist, this did not prevent occasional imagining, and very thorough imagining in workmanlike syntax. He thought this was how a chortling, injurious message from Mark might go:

Casp,
    You never answered my last, but perhaps it has been made obsolete by situational

shifts. We have here what might reasonably be termed a turn-up! Among many applications for an established staff Creating Writing post we advertised comes one from a Lucy Marie Corth whom I know you wot well of. I think I mentioned to you earlier that I try not to let poets anywhere near this campus owing to their special aptitudes in articulate malice, tantrums and obfuscation. These are, of course, qualities endemic in all university Arts Departments worth their salt and vinegary vinegar, but poets infuse extra. These *avant garde* days they bring neither rhyme nor reason. My suspicions of Corth would obviously be maximum in that she is not just a poet but a blazoned poet and one who in her application writes quite openly, brassily, of her successes. Normally, I would therefore let the C. W. Department know that this candidate should proceed as far as the short list – to display openmindedness and fair's fair – but no fucking further, thank you. We have an application, also, from the A. F. W. Ichbald you told of earlier, who, I gather, was also part of your C. W. venture there until the cull, and whose special area is mime and drama. By contrast, these are almost invariably OK interests since theatre writers have to be nice to directors and actors and so develop a kind of humanity which poets – alone, contemplative, twitchy and vile – don't. At another time, Ichbald's papers I might have given the nod to. We get initials only on Ichbald's application so I remain unenlightened on gender. Schools listed in his/her cv are all mixed.

However, the fact that Corth openly called you a cunt twice does clearly go some way to improve her image as against the usual sneaky poet's. And I remember your saying early on that she is a quite sensational piece physically, as well as all the rest of it, a judgement confirmed by several of our C. W. lads who have met her at conferences, and what are cheerfully referred to as 'Four-Day-Three-Night Writers' Retreats', in various spots around the country, including Droitwich, and fully subsidized from university funds. She claims on her cv to be twenty-five years old, which is not an age in women I have any fixed objection to. One of the C. W. males puts her height at 5' 6" or 7", which would probably unnerve you (though think of Micky Rooney) but not men taller than yourself, meaning most, including me.

Accordingly, Casp, I've decided to let it be intimated that T. L. S. Corth perhaps fits the bill rather than Ms/Mr Ichbald. I imagine this might mean we give her the job, since the selection committee is five men and one woman, at least four of the men hetero, and two of these under sixty and standardly avid, as well as possibly keen on verse and respectful of the *TLS*. In any impasse, I have the casting vote, naturally, and I would be prepared, given the exceptional factors, to endorse Corth, although flagrantly poetic.

All right, this was a make-believe message from Eider, and *only* make-believe, but Ballaugh considered it fairly feasible. Eider would think such tactics the most beautiful, infuriating jape. He must be stopped. Inevitably, then, Ballaugh became aware of a growing mass of factors pushing him towards the attempted reinstatement of Lucy Corth:

1) Mo and the City Of Culture – meaning:
2) the Government and the City Of Culture – meaning:
3) a possible peerage if the City of Culture title came.
4) Pressure from Dape re the City Of Culture.
5) Mark Eider and the flesh-creep prospect of his scooping Lucy up.

But, although that fanciful email brought re-
solve to Ballaugh's mind, it did not suggest
methods. How would he go about a repen-
tant crawl to Lucy? He did not think there
had been anything in those guides to business practice about the way to smarm someone you'd fired by mistake, who'd called you
a cunt twice at full voice in a public drinks
and canapé setting, and whom now, please,
oh please, you wanted to take her old job
back, as if her marching orders had been a
little mistake by Admin. Or Personnel.
Would Corth even look at the proposal? Did
she need to, post *TLS?*

Might she be more receptive if the offer
came from a go-between? Len Maldave remained the obvious means. He seemed to
befriend her on that difficult day, and perhaps more. Apparently, they left together.
Close? Very? Would he act as peacemaker
now? He'd want to keep her, wouldn't he?
But if she and Maldave were on matey
terms, he might have absorbed part of her
disgust for Ballaugh. That could be especially so if Maldave saw her possible move
away to Eider as actually *caused* by Ballaugh,
or Ballaugh and Mo in dire alliance. And this
would not be illogical. Another inconvenient

point: Ballaugh had wondered whether Len Maldave was the right person to represent the university on the City Of Culture Literary Committee – whether he had the drive and colourfulness. But Ballaugh could hardly in conscience replace him, humiliate and bruise him, if Maldave helped with Lucy. So, Ballaugh would be using Maldave to bring back Corth and strengthen the City Of Culture case while, at the same time, stuck with Maldave who, in Ballaugh's view, actually weakened the City Of Culture case.

God, the complexities hammered him, almost convinced Ballaugh he could do nothing effective about anything and should cower away somewhere and simply reflect on that one terrible, vainglorious step taken beyond his competence, to a Vice-Chancellorship; even to a Vice-Chancellorship in a place like this. But perhaps he had taken *more* than one step. However many he'd taken, he'd better not take any more. Should he simply go into withdrawal?

And then a further factor turned up, shoving him hard back towards action: that is, it forced him to decide some kind of diplomatic grovel to Lucy might yet be the necessary thing, the only thing, even the right thing. Ballaugh took a phone call from Gabriel, his younger son. Or rather, he took a call and then, as requested by Gabriel, rang back. In line with Fiona's edict, neither boy had gone into politics. Piers landed a job in the media, which she did not think nearly as bad, and where, in her view, there'd at least be a fair number of men called Piers, so he wouldn't get sniggered at. Gabriel, though, had had a series of tougher times and sad disasters and needed all the backing available. Ballaugh, a tender father, yearned to give it – did give it, when he could and as long as Gabriel stayed reasonably far off: some money, some encouragement, much affection, no actual articulated scream at Gabriel to get his fucking finger out. A failed coach driver; failed manicurist – talking of fingers; failed call centre operative; failed window-cleaner; and failed snooker hall maître d', Gabriel was at present blessedly, and almost unbelievably, more than four months through his trial spell for a dog warden career in Manchester. He seemed at last to be in a job he enjoyed and could hold. Ballaugh considered Gabriel had done splendidly to discover aged twenty-eight what his talents might be, and then go with what looked really damned like determination for this post. Ballaugh dialled the number.

'They don't like us having private calls

out,' Gabriel said.

'Who?'

'"A Dog's Life."'

'You really consider yours is still that, Gabriel?' Ballaugh asked, all his anxieties reignited. 'I thought you—'

'Name of the firm. Humorous, you know. The warden jobs are franchized to them by the city.'

'Oh. Is everything all right?'

'I was talking to Mum just now.'

'Mum as well? Your telephone day? Is it a quiet time there – I mean, the dogs?' Ballaugh replied. He could hear some of them barking mildly, well-adjustedly, in the background. He found it heartening that Manchester had this good facility for strays. This showed the city in a nicer light: it was not all drugs turf wars there with guns.

Gabriel said: 'Mum told me you might be up for a peerage. Gee, dad. *Lord* Ballaugh.'

'Rumour – and very fragile rumour at this stage. Really, she shouldn't be talking like that.' No, Fiona shouldn't.

'Great. You deserve it.'

'Thanks, Gabriel.' However ... yes, however and however. *However,* there'd been, hadn't there, that point-blank end to Mo's phone call explaining changed policy towards Lucy? It had been virtually 'Get

214

Corth'. Not quite *Get Carter*, the film title, but the same imperative crackle. Did Mo mean Ballaugh would certainly cop no peerage if he failed to bring her back, and bring her back fast, for the Culture drive? Of course he fucking meant that. This thought had already troubled Ballaugh. He'd been surprised at how much it *did* trouble him. There was something in Ballaugh – something minor, he hoped, but definitely present – something that fancied being the Lord of Vallin Court. This had a good ring to it, and sort of tied in with the history of the place. He certainly did not despise history, as he'd told members of that department in the university for their morale. In fact Ballaugh had told several departments he did not despise their subject, including Classics and Religious Studies, especially since they'd taken some of the cuts. These types of subject needed a little reassurance now and then. He didn't want staff pacing about, worriedly asking themselves, 'What am I for?' – except in Philosophy, perhaps, where this question could be the basis for at least a term's lectures, and possibly a doctoral thesis.

He believed a peerage need hardly be at variance with the Outreach principle that Mo expounded so fully when at the Court.

After all, as to reaching out, Ballaugh would actually *be* reaching out through his continued sponsorship of university Outreach, although a full Lord. He would be an Outreaching Lord, not one isolated and superior in his property. Surely, in some aspects this could be seen as more thoroughly for the people and democratic, rather than less. It would weaken class distinctions by creating a new one. Paradoxes did not scare Ballaugh, though you met few in economics. Besides, suddenly Mo and the Government seemed cool on Outreach. They wanted Up-reach. They desired a Culture City win. They craved that distinction, that élitism. Margaret Thatcher would have understood and fulsomely praised their turn-around.

'This could be the break, dad,' Gabriel said.

'In what sense, son?'

'My future.'

'I don't understand.'

'These things count for a lot.'

'Which?'

'Peerages and so on.'

'Only a formality,' Ballaugh said.

'What I thought – if you were a Lord, I'd be an Honourable, wouldn't I?'

'Probably. There's all kinds of mucking about in prospect for the House of Lords, you know. But, yes, as things stand you'd be the Honourable Gabriel Ballaugh.'

'Sounds great, like from a Walter Scott novel. Derring-do. Could be a real help with my prospects. There probably aren't many the Hons. in dog work.'

'Well, no, maybe not.'

'A promotion route exists – senior warden, principal warden, or even managerial appointments. It can possibly broaden out into animal pest control and amending Nature generally – pigeons, sea gulls, grey squirrels, cormorant culls, general vermin. Clout, dad. The Hon. would give me clout. Being an Hon. would get me at least through the paper-sifts for higher posts. I'd be more, like, professional.' Gabriel chuckled. Behind his voice came the sound of what might be a biggish dog – labrador, airedale? – getting well treated and spoken softly to by someone, and snuffling gratefully back. Gabriel said: 'When I mentioned "professional", I wouldn't want to scare anybody by seeming over-ambitious!'

'One must watch out for that.' Oh, God, yes.

'Professional! Big, big word!' Gabriel chuckled some more. 'Talking about professional, remember how mum used to fret, really, really fret, in case Piers or I became

217

professional politicians and made it to the Cabinet, dad?'

'Still does. You've managed somehow to dodge that slot, anyway – both picked your own vocations.'

'I feel I'm doing well in this new work. I see openings, if only I can get a little extra push, such as the Hon.' Self-assertion deepened his voice. 'I think I'm able to take an enlightened overview of this work. They're looking for that kind of inborn ability. For instance, it seems to me that as more and more local authorities ask householders to put rubbish out for collection in black plastic bags, the importance of removing roving dog packs before they can tear at them and create street hygiene problems in their search for food will become increasingly marked. Not to sound immodest, but I think I have vision in this realm. I believe I've had the good judgement to pick a growth occupation – steadier than politics. Important to stick with that. I expect you've noticed those animal welfare posters saying a puppy is more than a Christmas present, and must not be abandoned after the holiday. I'm happy to know I'm doing something about that problem.'

Gabriel might be correct. The work probably didn't pay as well as Mo's, but perhaps added up to more. The boy was settling. He, indeed, had vision. It would be cruel and absurd not to assist by getting him his fragment of the title, if possible. Additionally, Ballaugh had an abiding dread that if Gabriel's dog job fell through he might want to come and live at Vallin Court.

'I thought mum sounded much more content – happier – than lately,' Gabriel said. 'She told me she's looking around for new interests.'

'Well, yes.'

'Poetry.'

'Yes.'

'Modern style.'

'Yes.'

'The urban predicament.'

'That kind of thing.'

'Is it all right with you, dad?'

'Why not?'

'Some self-exposure involved? That's how poetry goes, isn't it, even the modern kind.'

'Fine by me.'

'Mum seems to be sort of finding herself.'

Ballaugh did not like that phrase. He'd used it – not favourably – in his head about women members of amateur drama groups with Elton Dape. Finding herself where? Under the uncuff-linked barfly? Under Mo? 'You were always fond of dogs, Gabriel,' Ballaugh said. 'It might well amount to a flair.'

'I think so, dad: like Menuhin with the violin. I believe I can reconcile the two apparently contradictory sides of this occupation at the higher levels. The two thematic strands.'

'Contradictory? Thematic?'

'The work with strays – positive, clearly humane, life-preserving: the aim is to return the animals to their owners or find new ones for them. And then on the other side, the pest control: this can be destructive, terminal. How to make these seemingly opposed aspects coalesce? It's a fair question, dad, and one I've given—'

'Your mother's truly delighted at the progress you're making, Gabriel,' Ballaugh replied.

'I'm glad. And she's quite excited about getting a title herself, you know, dad. She's so proud of you for having cleverly nabbed it, despite all these mad, devious Ministers and so on you have to satisfy and obey and butter.'

'Yes, I do plenty of that. It's an executive skill, nothing more – like reading a barometer. Routine. I mugged up the various ploys from a couple of books. But we haven't got it yet, you know.'

'What?'

'The peerage.'

'The subtlety and power you've shown in lining up this ennoblement for the family are the kinds of subtlety and power I'm looking for myself in the dog world and maybe even beyond, into that wider pest domain I spoke of, dad.'

'Excited? Is she?'

'She wouldn't show you, would she, in case it influenced your judgement on some topic or other to do with landing the peerage? She'd hate to seem to push you.'

She'd probably think Ballaugh so small because of his decline that if she did push him he'd tumble apart, like a thawing snowman. 'And she's proud, you say, Gabriel?'

'Very proud of you, dad. We all are.'

That sod in the bar wouldn't be able to offer her a title, nor Mo, yet. And if she were a Lady it wouldn't be appropriate for her to go trawling night spots, clearly. Spouting at Outreach jamborees about experiencing experiences in experienced sheets would be out, too; or about dreaming of experiencing experiences in experienced sheets.

'Only two more months and I'll have graduated to full wardenship, a true feature of the hierarchy,' Gabriel said. 'Manchester is an increasingly lively city, catching up fast on London in amenities. It's good here, dad.

The Hon. will really set me up that bit better.'

'Right, Gabriel. Onwards. We're with you. I'll try to clinch it.'

And Ballaugh would. He decided he must definitely persuade Lucy Corth back, for all the reasons previously niggling him and these new ones: Corth might help get the City of Culture award, which might help Ballaugh get his university into the select Russell group, which might help him land the peerage, which might help keep Gabriel successful and distant and help keep Fiona away from poetry and flophouse beds.

But he would try the approach to Lucy in his own informal way, at least for now. He might see if he could set up an apparently accidental meeting and hope something positive could develop from there. A compromise: the business manuals believed in compromises. On balance, he'd found he did not much fancy asking Maldave to middleman. This was not the kind of relationship a Vice-Chancellor should have with one of his staff. If Maldave refused, and put the word around that he'd been asked, it would make Ballaugh look sly and pathetic, and of course Maldave *would* put the word around. If Maldave accepted and it worked with Lucy, he'd still put the word around, claiming he had done what Ballaugh couldn't. This must damage his authority as Vice-Chancellor. Maldave might proclaim on the campus and elsewhere that he, personally, had brightened the city's chances in the Culture competition, countering a catastrophic error made or condoned by Ballaugh. Maldave would hint at an instinctive understanding between great writers, Corth and himself, something Ballaugh could not participate in.

He called up Lucy Corth's Personnel dossier on the screen and found the address of her flat. What he thought he would do was drive over there and park at a spot from which he could watch the front door. When she came out, he'd leave the car and behave as if he just happened to be walking by. Lately, he saw Michael Caine up to something of this sort in a TV rerun of the film, *Hannah And Her Sisters*. Caine, married to Hannah, falls for one of those sisters – a delicate situation – and wants to bring about this supposedly chance encounter. He has to dash around the block so as to confront her head-on, and Ballaugh might also need to do something similar. He was shorter than Caine, but most likely Ballaugh should have no trouble running a little distance, and still have breath to talk significantly.

Of course, Lucy Corth would probably

realize he had actually planned this seeming fluke. Why the hell else would he be walking in that part of the city? But he thought the obviousness of his ploy could be a help, not the reverse. She would see he was willing to put himself out for her sake. She would see he knew there had been a misjudgement and looked for a way to correct it, yet without utterly humbling himself. Poets lived by sensitivity, didn't they? Well, she could show a bit towards Ballaugh now. She'd had her moment of cursing him while standing high on a chair, the tall, vengeful bitch. He liked the idea of lurking in a car, watching. It brought a private eye or Secret Service flavour. This tactic would hardly appear in any business books, nor in the usual run of Vice-Chancellor duties. He could not be confined by the dull, standard requirements of a mere executive job. He was Caspar Ballaugh. He would live up to that, wouldn't he? Would he?

Today, he had a lunch engagement with Elton Dape and Ballaugh thought that, after it, he would drive to where Corth lived and start his surveillance. Ballaugh still felt irritated with Dape, city chief executive, am. dram. star, iron pumper, Francophile, woman fancier. All right, he had overall charge of the Culture campaign, but it still lay outside his role to contact Mo's Government office about reinstatement of Corth. This was a university matter, a Ballaugh matter, and he meant to tell Dape so. *'Boundaries, Elton,'* he'd say. *'Demarcation. Protocol.'* Of course, Dape would want to know what had been done about getting Corth on board again since he and Ballaugh last spoke. Ballaugh thought he would not disclose his private scheme to re-recruit her. If Dape heard of that the sod would assume his phone call to Mo's office had led to more pressure on Ballaugh, and his *volte face*. Dape's phone call to Mo's office *had* led to more pressure on Ballaugh, and part produced his *volte face*, but he'd like to keep Dape from crowing about that, just as he'd like to keep Maldave from crowing about *his* influence in the Corth crisis. Ballaugh had his dignity to preserve, the dignity of office and, possibly, of a Lordship. He'd be up there in ermine with Falconer and Kinnock. He wouldn't want some baroness edging up to him to say, 'You're the one that French-spouting twat Elton Dape owns, aren't you?'

Dape, hosting the lunch, did not leap right into the Corth situation, or not obviously he didn't. For a while he seemed to want to discuss his theatre side. There'd be some dirty purpose, though, and Ballaugh tried to work out what actually was happening. Over the *hors d'oeuvres* at Tim's Brasserie, Dape said: 'Not Lear. Not yet, at any rate. I don't think I'm altogether ready for him.'

'It's always vital to know one's range,' Ballaugh replied. Oh, God, yes.

'Make-up could give me the age well enough. It's not so much that. No, but I feel there are parts I could take on more naturally, effortlessly: Prince Hal, Jimmy Porter – that's *Look Back In Anger,* you know.'

'Actually, I look *forward* in confidence to those,' Ballaugh said waggishly, despite everything. Elton had such a soaring sense of himself that Ballaugh felt it would be inhuman not to go along with it in part.

'Oh, this is all very amateur, believe me, Caspar, I'm ever aware of that. Can't have any relevance for our City Of Culture drive.' He pondered. 'Or Coriolanus. The grandiosity of him. *L'orgueil.* In some ways a highly dubious figure, admittedly. Yet this is what helps make him rounded, isn't it?'

'I—'

'Tell me, do you see what's the common quality in all the characters I've spoken of, Casp – Lear, Hal, Jimmy Porter, Coriolanus? Especially Coriolanus.'

'Well, they're all male – not Widow Twankey parts.'

226

'Power, Casp.'

'Right.'

'Power.'

So, was this it? Did Dape mean over the liver and bacon main to reveal some special facet of his power, some unpleasantly relevant facet of his power? Ballaugh felt sure Dape had a bundle of relevant facets, most of them unpleasant. Ballaugh held back for a while the planned snarl about Elton's intrusive nose poking via Mo's office. Ballaugh needed to know more about this Dape power, and how it might fuck him up if Dape decided he, Ballaugh, had better be fucked up in a Dape cause, the only cause that Dape would fully recognize.

'Power – its exercise, its perils, its potential for good and for evil – fascinates me,' Dape said.

Even if the word had not come at the beginning of a sentence, Ballaugh thought he would have sensed a capital P. He seemed to recall the local paper said of Dape's Antony that it was 'intermittently imperious', which, for some creepy upper city hall clerk, had to be regarded as OK. Ballaugh did not like Tim's Brasserie. It tried for rough-and-readiness, and managed an ambience some way below a very dodgy Routiers' caff in France. Of course, the French element would charm Ballaugh. On top of that, Ballaugh had the notion Dape brought him here to show he didn't have to care about appearances or refinements because his position, authority, personality could between them do all the necessary. Cheap cutlery took on distinction in his hands. Power.

'Power,' Dape said. *'Puissance.'* He got his jaw into granite mode, although eating. 'You'll reply that you can see the Power significance of Lear, Hal, Coriolanus, because they are obvious leaders, or a potential leader in the case of Hal, who, of course, became Henry the Fifth. Lear sheds Power. Hal schemes for it. Coriolanus fights for it. But Jimmy Porter? A young man. Power? Yes, I regard Porter, and *Look Back In Anger*, as centrally about Power. It's domestic Power in his case, the need for dominance.' He waved his fifty pence fork, but disarmingly. 'I do go on and on. How are things with you, Casp?'

Ballaugh said: 'Oh, look, Elton, I wanted to—'

'As to young men, I was hearing about *your* lad, *your* Prince Hal, your Gabriel, the other day,' Dape replied.

'Oh?'

'One of these senior local Government officer get-together things – on a national basis. Gabriel's in Manchester?'

'A probationary job.'

'I gathered. His boss was at this do. Nice fellow, Oliver. A real magnifico in the abatement of nuisance game, an equivalent to Red Adair who used to quell oilfield fires. Ollie goes all over the world. Tasmania, Peru, India, advising. Not just stray dogs. Known him from way back. Oh, way, way back. Well, I'd mentioned you in conversation, apropos the Culture campaign here – your valued participation. Not a common surname. And Oliver said that, oddly, he had a talented boy working for him in the dog house called Ballaugh. Two and two were put together, you see. Oliver told me he'd heard the boy's father was big in university administration somewhere. I could enlighten him – and, naturally, asked Ollie to keep a benevolent eye on Gabriel. And, from a distance, I will myself, of course, Casp.'

Power. Ballaugh saw what the build up had been about: Dape could be a powerhouse on stage, and also a powerhouse influence in the real and expanding domain of civic pest control, Gabriel's fine and only *métier*. The boy needed all the leverage possible in his late-burgeoning work scene. One day, with the right help he might be invited to Tasmania, Peru and India himself advising

on more than dogs, the Hon. Gabriel Ballaugh, dispensing short shrift to global pests.
There'd be no further danger then that
Gabriel might flop again and want to come
and live with Ballaugh and Fiona.

He opted now to forget about Dape's
intervention with Mo. After all, he *wanted*
Dape's intervention with Oliver for Gabriel.
Ballaugh would love some of Dape's power
to be used for the boy, whether the Lear
type, the Prince Hal type, the Coriolanus
type, or the Jimmy Porter type. Just let it
work. Please, LET IT FUCKING WORK.
'I'm going to try to get Lucy Corth back,
Elton,' he said, around some halibut. It was
only confirmation of what he'd already
settled in his head, but now the decision had
been placed immutably on record, and it
acknowledged a bargain between Dape and
him.

'This will require a plan,' Dape said.

Christ, after Coriolanus he could play
Eisenhower at D-Day.

'Have you a scheme, Casp?'

'Nothing formulated quite yet. But that's
only a question of detail.'

'Speed – of some significance now. I hear
the city might have been shortlisted.'

'Yes? Grand. You've done brilliantly, Elton.'

'A team thing. We'll be under scrutiny. We

must excel. And this girl excels. I don't mean her body and so on. *La poésie*. Her lovely way with words.'

'She called me a cunt,' Ballaugh said.

'There could be a positive side to that.'

'Yes?'

'Oh, certainly. Many women feel they should unashamedly esteem that part of themselves.'

'It didn't sound like esteem. *Rapprochement* might be tricky.'

'I said to Oliver, "Some have a gift for dogs, some not,"' Dape replied, '"and it seems to me, Ollie, from what you tell me, that young Gabriel outstandingly has. Outstandingly." True, I said, I'd never met Gabriel but I could sense from his words – I mean Ollie's – that he – I mean Gabriel – would never wilfully torment a dog of any known breed for mere kicks. Yes, I remarked, this was a gift of nature, but it must also be nurtured and given its chance to flourish and flourish. I mentioned all this to Oliver, and will certainly be mentioning it to him again when we're in touch, which we often are, in the course of things, Casp, obviously.'

'Well, thanks, Elton.' Sometimes, Ballaugh thought Fiona might be depressingly, cruelly, right and he really had started to dwindle. God, to be sucking up to a slick, featherbedded wordster like Dape. Only someone measly, or well on the way to measly, could contemplate that.

'Should, perhaps, *I* make the approach?' Dape said.

'To Lucy Corth?' Keep fucking well out of things, you Lear-in-waiting and Coriolanus clone – keep out of things, except things that might help Gabriel, such as the occasional purposeful lean on Ollie, your good pal.

Dape said: 'If she thought the *city* wanted her, as distinct from, or as well as, the university – not that this is in any way to downplay the status of the university – hardly! Would I? – but if, via one's self, she came to realize how much I, personally, and the city—'

'I do think this is the kind of thing I should arrange myself, in the circumstances.'

'Not to diminish your potential effectiveness in the least, Caspar, but for a young girl like that to be singled out by someone in my post, with my responsibilities and, I trust, civic spirit – yes, to be singled out by someone in my post, representing, I think I can reasonably claim, this great conurbation and this great conurbation's intents – do you not feel that this might impress, might convince her that her role is unquestionably with us, despite previous ... previous ... previous, well, unfortunate *contretemps*?'

'She can be fiery.'

'I realize that, could hardly *not* realize it, Casp, in view of her shouts at—'

'But you said these cunt-cries were accolades. She would see an intercession by you, Elton, as roundabout – a side-step by me, a rather demeaning trick.'

'There'd be no trick. I'd say to her: "We admire you, Lucy. We need you, Lucy. You are unique, Lucy, and the very uniqueness carries a duty."' Dape put grand resonance into these words, and anyone could have told he took major power figures on stage. They should re-title that play for him to *Look Back In Clangour*. 'She would not object to use of her first name, Casp. They're like that in the arts. If, as you say, you have no formulated scheme for approaching her, why not let me take over?'

'I think I'd better do it, at least in the first instance, Elton.'

'Dresden, Palermo – these are our shortlist rivals. There can't be delays, Casp.'

'I appreciate this.'

And he did. On his way towards Lucy Corth's street and flat, that thrill of urgency, subterfuge and secrecy took a happy grip on Ballaugh. He felt like a John le Carré figure in authentic Cold War days. Why should

233

Dape be the only one to get theatrical? Ballaugh saw himself not as a royal, or an angry young tyrant, or a dictator, though, but as an undercover man. Yes, one of Smiley's people: polished, necessarily furtive, subtle, tough. He glanced often in the car mirror to check whether Dape was, in fact, tailing him to find what he would do about Corth. A ludicrous idea, but in his present state the notion excited him, seemed of a pattern with the general atmosphere of stealth and dubious promise.

At a good spot for watching the front door of her flat block, he sank very low in the seat of his car so as not to be recognized if she came out. He thought his eyes probably shone sharp and formidable, though not ruthless, but he didn't want to sit up to check in the mirror because that might make him obvious. While waiting, he worked out some words to try on her, suppose he got the chance. This was a poet and he knew he must avoid cliché phrases such as 'let bygones be bygones', or Blair's 'draw a line under', or 'we all make mistakes'. When she was one of his Creative Writing staff she would probably put a red ink ring around such shagged-out expressions. Yes, oh, God, *when* she was. But he would say nothing to Corth that tried to disown Mo and claim it had been *his* decision to fire Lucy and A. F. W. Ichbald, so absolving himself. He would *like* to say that, and he more than half believed it true, but he must not dodge. No bucks should be passed, talking of clichés. There was a collective responsibility. The business manuals had sharp chapters on collective responsibility. Lucy obviously believed Ballaugh did the damage, or she would not have aimed her attack at him, rather than at Education and its politicians, generally.

He thought something positive must come from him like: 'Lucy, we don't want to lose you. We esteem you. In a sense, of course, we already *have* lost you, since your contract has been terminated. But this termination can itself be terminated! Oh, you will no doubt rejoin that my sudden wish to keep you after all is the result of your achievements elsewhere, namely the *TLS*. And it would be foolish for me to deny this is a factor in the invitation to you now. I can say only that your talent was always obvious but its glittering confirmation in the *Literary Supplement* brings home to someone who is, after all, no expert on literary concerns, only a diligent economist, the full range of that talent, and it would be perverse if I did not offer at once to rectify our error by asking you to take up a renewed contract – but now a tenured contract – with us.' Wordy? Not half. But he'd push on. 'I know I speak for other staff and all C. W. students.'

Ballaugh would have wished to give Lucy a tenured post, anyway, but especially because, in the imagined email from Eider, that calculating sod had spoken of an established staff appointment, or would have if he'd written the email, and might still if she did go to his team. Ballaugh reckoned Lucy's poetic abilities should bring credit to the university for decades, not just in the Culture City run-up, no matter how her looks and general shape might slip with age. Of course, he saw the possibility that she might simply keep walking today, refuse to hear him, act as if she had not even noticed him, like Alida Valli striding scornfully past Joseph Cotten at the end of *The Third Man*, and he'd be reciting this peace formula to himself in the street. Then, it might be necessary to commission Len Maldave and hope he would not respond with a similar brush-off. Ballaugh must certainly persist somehow should he be snubbed today – or whenever he could contrive the meeting. He, naturally, preferred to think she would show him magnanimity, and acknowledge he had come up with a rare deal: universities did not chuck long-term contracts around these days, despite what Eider said, or might have said in the email, if there'd been one, or might yet say.

Lucy Corth appeared in the little front porch of the flat block. She was with a man, though, a man Ballaugh did not recognize: tall, dark haired, young-to-youngish, wearing a navy pea-jacket, jeans and brown cowboy boots. All right, a complication, but if this was her live-in he, too, had better hear what Ballaugh would say. He reached out and put his hand on the door handle, ready to leave the car as soon as they showed which way she would go. He stayed low in his seat for the moment, though, or they might notice movement. The tension authenticated him: he was a secret operative. She had on blue cord trousers and a suede jacket worn open. Fair haired, energetic, slim, she stood very straight and gazed down the road to her left as if expecting someone or something. She carried a green canvas briefcase. The man had a leather rucksack on his back. Ballaugh thought again how, with such looks, she would be grossly wasted in a place like Wales and near someone like Mark Eider. Oddly, it was not the word 'beautiful' that came first to his mind as description of her – though she *was* beautiful – but 'vivid': he meant the liveliness of her face and the golden flash of her hair now and then in the off-and-on spells of sun. She went beyond poetry, even poetry in the *TLS*. She was womanhood. Perhaps he should have realized she would not be living alone.

A Mercedes taxi drew up. Fuck, they didn't mean to walk. Fuck, he must try to gumshoe her motorized, as he recently thought Dape might be gumshoeing *him*. Ballaugh had seen car tailing done, but only in the cinema or on TV. He knew it would be much more tricky than appeared there. Or much more tricky for him. He lacked the training. He was an economist and Vice-Chancellor. All the same, he sat up properly behind the wheel and when the taxi moved off with Corth and friend in the back he tried to get behind. How *exactly* was it done on screen? Did you aim to put your own vehicle right on the back bumper of the quarry, or follow with two or three other cars between, for cover? In fact, though, he did not have that choice. He had parked in a side street and couldn't get out and into the traffic flow on this bigger road until three cars passed. He joined the string then. For about five minutes he kept the taxi intermittently in sight. But at the big Baine's Bridge roundabout it went out of view behind the fucking dense and high environmental foliage, and by the time Ballaugh reached there it was impossible to know which of three exits the Mercedes took.

Ballaugh chose the second and did not see the taxi again. He felt incompetent, doomed, but that canvas briefcase pleased him. It was an economy job. She still needed to look after her money. He had a three-division, double-lock briefcase in high calibre leather. It came with the Vice-Chancellorship. That cut-price thing of Corth's made her seem weak, reclaimable, bribable.

What was *in* her briefcase? Further damn poems? Would she get another tranche of *gloire* from somewhere significant, making the amputation of her from the department still dafter, more perverse? But whom would they be taking them to? Why the taxi? Might the case contain samples of her work for somebody? For Eider? Perhaps the Merc went to the station. One exit from Baine's Bridge roundabout led there, though not the one he'd opted for. Ballaugh picked another route to the trains now, parked and bought a platform ticket. He ran up the steps to where she and the man would have to wait supposing their destination Wales, and stared about. If he hunted them down here he would certainly not be able to pretend the meeting was accidental. So? He just wanted to locate her. He would say something constructive and pleasant about the briefcase, praising its colour and overall unusualness as compared with all the dull, official black and brown leather versions. But would she regard such chatter as lunatic and a ploy from someone she'd called a cunt? *Would* such chatter be lunatic and a ploy? Of course it would.

He didn't find them, though. Possibly the train had gone. He must have arrived a long while after the taxi. Possibly she never came here. He wondered at what point panic moved into breakdown. How had the briefcase looked? Did it seem well-filled, say with overnight stuff as well as poems? If she were on her way to Wales it would probably be for an interview tomorrow. Yes, he thought the briefcase had shown a certain bulk, and so did the rucksack. It disturbed him to think her work portfolio might have been pushed against a change of underwear in her brief-case – *brief*case – and that Mark Eider would soon be looking at it, handling it – that is, the portfolio, at this stage.

He gave up and in the evening did a trudge looking for the poetic bar in Fiona's poem. He knew some of the city centre pubs, already, of course. None of these had such a mirror and he could eliminate them from his search. It had sounded like a place where office staffs and possibly lawyers and bank employees went after work and maybe lingered, so he concentrated on the business streets of the centre. At his third call, he did see at the far end of the premises a mirror brightly illuminated from below. Between it and the door, noisy, well-dressed people sat and stood, perhaps drinking their bonuses. Most were men, and Ballaugh could imagine a woman would feel their eyes on her if she walked the length of the place to rendezvous with a lover at the mirror, as in Fiona's lines. Some women would not care for that very much, or would at least *say* they didn't care for it, but Fiona made this out to be a brilliant extra to the rest of the evening, a taster.

He went in and took a stool at the counter before the mirror. Generally he drank beer or wine but didn't consider either of these fitted the kind of hard-living, attractively unjoyful profile he wanted here, and he ordered Cointreau. In the mirror, he thought he looked podgy just under his jaw and on each side of his nose above the mouth. Podginess was no good at all for what he wanted. Podginess made him appear childlike and therefore hardly capable of the mature, long-term disappointment and pain which would make his face so sombrely fascinating, a

241

Hopper face.

It was not a Friday, but he wondered what would happen should Fiona come in and find him sitting there alone. The answer to that must be that if she entered the pub and spotted him she would turn around and disappear, realizing why he had turned up and not wishing to confirm he interpreted the poem correctly. Interpret, for God's sake? Did it *need* interpreting? It had vicious, appalling clarity. Probably she would abandon the evening, although this implied no experiences in the experienced sheets and no responsive flesh-glow as she became an eyeful trekking through the bar from the street door. That situation seemed unlikely because the poem said she arrived *after* the ill-natured male, although, of course, it might refer only to the one horribly specific night which inspired her to appallingly confessional Outreachery verse.

A man came and took the stool next to him in front of the mirror. They nodded at each other in it. He was long faced, craggy, tall, strong jawed, unmoustached, no hat, hair grey-dark. He had on a good navy suit and open-necked white shirt. Ballaugh couldn't at first make out whether he wore cuff-links. 'Only the valiant take these seats,' he said.

'Why?' Ballaugh asked.

'One has to look at one's self.'

'There are worse people to look at,' Ballaugh replied. 'In any case, what you see there isn't what others see when they look at you because the mirror reverses things.'

'That right?'

'But you can still get some comfort from looking at yourself.'

'Is that what you're after?'

'What?' Ballaugh replied.

'Comfort.'

'I like to do an inventory.'

'Of?'

'See it's all reasonably as it was. One's appearance, for what it's worth. A morale thing.'

'Women like it.'

'What?' Ballaugh asked.

'Sitting here.'

'Why?'

'Well, one, they can check they're as good as they can get as to make-up and hair. Two, they will watch the blokes without being too blatant about it, and be ready with whatever response they fancy if they see someone eyeing them and maybe about to come over.' He ordered brandy and another Cointreau for Ballaugh. When he reached for the brandy, Ballaugh saw the shirt had white buttons, not cuff-links. Worrying – especially as the man was also trilbyless. 'Should we be sitting here, then?' Ballaugh said.

'Why not?'

'Taking their places.'

'Whose?'

'The women's.'

'They're not on the game, mind.'

'No, bars don't like that.'

'But they're aware – the women, that is.'

'Of what?' Ballaugh said.

'I've met one or two very nice women here.'

'Which?'

'What?'

'One or two?' Ballaugh asked.

'For instance, I don't know if you're going to be around for a while tonight, no commitments.'

'Why?'

'Well, taking your point, we could go and sit over there with the high-fliers and execs and wait to see what turns up. We've warmed the stools for them.'

'Is there any day, or rather night, that's better in this bar than others?' Ballaugh asked.

'In what sense?'

'When aware women, or an aware woman, alone, is more likely to show,' Ballaugh said.

'Really, most women, if they look anything at all, are aware all the time, aren't they?'

'No special day?'

'For experiences?'

'Yes, experiences,' Ballaugh said. 'You've hit it.'

They were silent for a time. Ballaugh ordered him another brandy but did not take a third Cointreau. He knew this to be against drinking protocol – conferring a cheap round on himself – but he had begun to think he might have made a mistake in coming here.

'About what time?' Ballaugh asked,

'What?'

'If they're coming. What time do they show? The women. Or a woman,' Ballaugh said.

'I don't mind all that much if none of them arrive.'

'Who?' Ballaugh asked.

'Women. I can just sit here and get so I feel solitary and yet significant. Do you know a painter called Hopper?'

'Hopper?'

'American. Edward.'

'No,' Ballaugh said.

'He did people like you and me – lonely, young-to-middle-aged turds getting friendly with the only one who wants to get friendly with them, which is themselves, via a mirror. The booze helps, naturally. They – we – stare at the glass and, as the drink does its nice little job, they – we – think they – we – look ill-used but full of a grand history and a grand potential for ... for experience.'

'What I wondered was if, say, Fridays were especially hot,' Ballaugh replied.

'Hot in which way?'

'The women.'

'I don't like a word like "hot" for it. These can be quite classy pieces, decent scent and capped teeth.'

'Scent?'

'Oh, yes.'

'From which part of the body?'

'What?'

'The scent. Forearms?'

'They're aware, yes, but not tangling their legs with yours right off on the stools, and that kind of rapid, invasive thing.'

'Friday's not particular then?'

'It's easier to get a room Fridays and weekends, because the reps and so on have gone home and the B. and B.s are keen for business.'

'So Fridays *could* be special?' Ballaugh asked.

'What's with you, if you don't mind my asking? What's the Friday thing?'

'I think I'll move along now,' Ballaugh replied.

'It's been an experience talking to you. But there are experiences and experiences, aren't there?'

Eleven

Of course, Len Maldave was keyed up waiting, and as soon as Lucy Corth rang the bell
of his flat he hurried to greet her. The hall
mirror showed him the vast welcoming grin
on his face as he passed. And he did really
struggle to keep the grin in place when he
opened the door and saw she had a man with
her. Lucy raised one hand and pointed it at
the tall, over-intelligent-looking, over-friend-
ly-looking stranger in an expensive navy blue
pea-jacket: coarse cloth, as required, but
splendidly cut. 'Len, I've brought Jeb Quarl,'
she said. 'Jeb, here's Len.'

Behind her and Jeb, a Mercedes taxi drew
away from the kerb. Did she usually get
around the city by taxi, not bus? Had the
TLS coughed up? But everyone knew poetry
didn't pay – except for real rocket-away
talents like Betjeman, Heaney, Cope,
Hughes. Or perhaps she'd decided she had
to put on a bit of a show and prove she
wasn't totally down after the sacking and

College Collage reception outburst. She might have raided her savings.

Or – another perhaps – perhaps dear Jeb paid. He had a chic rucksack on his back. These items – the pea-jacket and rucksack – might be his attempt to mingle the rough-and-ready and the fine, like knee-out Calvin Klein jeans. He seemed a taxi person – the kind who, by aura and profile, could ensure a For Hire cab would show just when he wanted one. He would fling the designer rucksack on to the back seat while snarling some very OK destination to the driver. In the hand not pointing at him, Lucy carried that green canvas briefcase Len had often seen her with around the university corridors, so at least she hadn't splashed out on a proper leather job, to suit the new reputation of her work. It wouldn't be *her* work in the case now, though, it would be *his*, wouldn't it?

'Jeb was apprehensive about coming with me, but I said, No need at all, you'd love to meet him.'

'So right if he's a pal of yours,' Maldave said, giving a true-false, welcoming handshake. Jeb would be about thirty, high-boot-ed, expertly coiffed, his teeth obviously all his own, almost certainly hetero, damn it.

'I'd really hate to intrude on what is bound

249

to be a conjoint literary session, Len,' Quarl said.

An American. Christ, the way they took over our language! Conjoint! 'Not at all, Jeb,' Maldave replied.

They went into the sitting room. To Maldave, Jeb looked like someone acting out the concept 'loose-limbed'. This was the way to move into someone's sitting room. Of course, Elaine would have loved his style. He had long, thin hands, the kind used to receiving good dollar dividend cheques, or checks. Maldave thought he'd seen people of Jeb's stamp being smilingly gracious to doormen in top hats and regalia outside London hotels favoured by Americans, such as the Connaught and Brown's.

'Something very weird, Len,' Lucy said.

'Yea, Lucy was really nonplussed,' Quarl said.

Maldave considered this sounded crudely familiar, almost intimate. It went beyond the easy use of her first name by Quarl. What right had he to speak of her nonplussedness, if there really had been nonplussedness? How could he be privy to her nonplussedness? To Maldave, nonplussedness did not seem an appropriate quality to stick on Lucy. Nothing with a 'non' in front would do for her. She was so positive.

'Weird?' Maldave asked.

'The Vice-Chancellor,' Lucy replied.

'Caspar Ballaugh? What about him?' Maldave said.

'I might be wrong.'

'Lucy couldn't be *totally* sure, but almost,' Quarl said. He knew how to track small gradations of her thoughts?

'Wrong in what way?' Maldave replied. He'd excitedly put out a tray with a bottle of Pouilly Fumé and two glasses. He went into the kitchen for a third glass.

'Sorry to upset the catering,' Jeb said.

Flippant sod. 'Glad you could come,' Maldave replied. And if Jeb was somehow a condition of Lucy's arrival, Maldave meant it, regardless. Anything: he felt so grateful to see her here. He'd grown certain Lucy would forget or ditch her interest in him and his letter novel, *In Times Of Broken Light*, now she'd landed such *TLS* recognition. That previous visit to his flat seemed like a different era – the day when she came here with him after the *College Collage* incident, and went over some of *In Times Of Broken Light*. It had all been so delightful then, and, apparently, so heartening for the future. She'd taken a copy of the script away, promising to work on it. And he certainly believed she would have done that, if there had not been this sudden deep change in things. He'd recognized he could not really expect her to stick with that promise now. Lucy was no longer merely an aggrieved, frantic, foul-mouthed sackee from the Creative Writing Department. Suddenly, she'd hit stardom. And stars shone and kept their distance. He had heard nothing, and, once the *TLS* transformed her, hadn't really expected to hear anything.

Or heard nothing until breakfast this morning when she telephoned to see whether he'd be at home and said she'd like to call in straight after lunch with her ideas for *In Times Of Broken Light*. He'd told her he had no class until the late afternoon and would be here. You bet he would be. *Lucy Come Home*. What she didn't say was that with her would be fit American Jeb. They sat down and took some of the wine. Maldave would have to be careful because of his teaching at four p.m. Quarl put the rucksack on the carpet at the side of his chair. It sat there like an obedient, richly brown dog, except for the zips. Rucksacks in general had become sinister since the London train and bus bombs, but this one looked benign, chummy.

'Yes, weird,' Lucy said.

'Concerning Ballaugh?' Maldave said.

'Do you know what kind of car he drives?' she asked.

'An Audi? Yes, the university supplies V-Cs with an Audi, I think.'

'An Audi,' she replied, nodding.

'Black.'

'Black Audi, right, Lucy,' Jeb said. 'You've got it right.' He sounded thrilled at her sharpness in deducing whatever it was she'd deduced. Jubilant. Perhaps the sod should be called Jub.

'I think he waited outside my place, watching from a parked black Audi, about ten past two,' Lucy said. 'Sunk low in the driver's seat, trying to stay unseen. Like sur-veil-lance? But I was looking down on him from my window, the way I was looking down on him from on the chair at the *College Collage* event. The porkiness of the face in the Audi seemed familiar and made me glance twice, and then some more. He tried to follow the taxi, like a cops drama.'

'Absolutely,' Jeb said.

'I told the driver to put his foot down at the big roundabout and we lost him,' Lucy said. 'I *think* we lost him.'

'I'm pretty sure,' Jeb said. 'A real polished tactic. Remember the way Lou, the Turk's driver in *Godfather One*, brilliantly swings the car around to defeat tails when they're taking Michael Corleone to the Italian restaurant? This was that standard.'

'It might not do you any good if Ballaugh knew I came here, Len. I'm a foe, aren't I? You'd get a quota of guilt by association.'

'Let me assure you, this concern for you really occupied Lucy's thoughts, Len,' Jeb said.

And the genial jerk made it sound as if he couldn't understand why. Maldave said: 'Or perhaps he doesn't regard you as a foe any longer, Lucy. There'd be no point in tailing you if he still sees you as that.'

'You think?'

'Likely.'

'Why?'

'He probably wants you back in the department.'

'You think?'

'He might have hoped to bump into you in the street, like by chance, and then he could start his sweet talk. Did you ever see that Michael Caine film where he fancies his sister-in-law and contrives an "accidental" meeting?'

'One of Woody Allen's best,' Jeb said. 'They go into a book shop and Caine reads love poetry to her. e. e. cummings?'

Fucking know-all. Cinema must be big with him: *Godfather One*, then recognizing

Hannah And Her Sisters. He didn't look the kind who'd have a big bag of popcorn at the movies – not someone in a pea-jacket like that – but you could never tell with Americans. Maldave loved that line in cummings about the girl with 'small important breasts'. Lucy's were just important, though.

'I wouldn't expect Caspar Ballaugh to read poetry to me,' Lucy said.

'Well, you write your own, don't you, Lucy?' Quarl said. 'Don't need it.'

'Ballaugh's pride would be involved,' Maldave said. 'He can't approach you direct, Lucy. And he has to be secretive, tactful, at this stage, so as not to appear abject, undignified. Probably he's been ordered by the Minister to countermand the sacking prontoest.'

'Minister Mo, Maurice, Theel decides university policy, Jeb,' Lucy said.

'I guessed that,' he replied.

Fucking know-all. 'Ballaugh will see it all as rather pressing,' Maldave said. 'There's the City Of Culture campaign. Possibly he's scared you'll take a job somewhere else. Well, he'd *definitely* be scared. He'll know you could have your pick now.'

He tried to speak it in a tone that asked her to deny she might be thinking of moving away. It gave him such pleasure to see her sitting there in one of his armchairs, the cut-price briefcase on her quality lap. That pleasure came even though Jeb sat in another of the armchairs and seemed to have some sort of link with her. Len would support the V-C. He yearned for Lucy to take her job back and stay.

'Jeb is part of Ingleby and Quarl Publishing, New York, Len.'

'Very much the second and subordinate part,' Quarl said. Modesty thrummed. But it sounded like a full partnership, just the same.

'Plus a London office and one in Sydney,' Lucy said. 'He was visiting London and happened to see a *TLS*.'

'Made a couple of phone calls to trace her. Jumped on a train,' Quarl said. 'Flung some stuff in my ever-faithful rucksack.' He tapped it fondly with his left boot. No explosion. 'Must see this out-of-nowhere poet. Find whether she'd ever done a collection. If other work existed. She's an obvious one for us.'

Would an American publisher rush like that to see Outreach writing? It was several days and nights since the *TLS* with Lucy's stuff in it came out. Jeb 'jumped on a train', did he? Was that immediate? Where had he been jumping since, and on whom? Maldave tried to work out if more than talent spotting, and *being* talent spotted, linked these two. He had been hoping to tune into concealed, hormonal signals to him personally in whatever new letters Lucy had written for *In Times Of Broken Light*: she'd said the script needed more sex, hadn't she? Instead, he found himself sniffing desperately at the chat from Lucy and Jeb, checking for give-away intimacies and rumpy-tumpy clues. Maldave would not have called him good looking, and not even not bad looking, but he had the idea most other people would find Jeb at least not bad looking and even *good* looking, including, possibly, Lucy.

So, idling through the *TLS*, this youthful publishing mogul is hit by her verse, hurtles here to meet her, maybe with a contract ready in his rucksack, then finds a stupendous face, a sublime body on the end of the stupendous, sublime poems: wouldn't that be almost incredibly wondrous for a recruiting, prospecting, talent-garnering Jeb? This was poetry made flesh.

Jeb said: 'Yes, Lucy thinks she'll come to us for US publication. Terrific. We're a fairly small house, sure, but it means we can give our authors and poets close personal attention.'

Yes, Maldave could fucking imagine.

Jeb said: 'The seven *TLS* poems, obviously, and another twenty or thereabouts. We've plenty to choose from, haven't we, Lucy?'

'Some will need a little work,' she said.

'Sure. But they exist, that's the chief thing,' Quarl said. 'We'll have a tremendous launch.' He turned to look at Maldave now, his voice still full of deference and admiration: 'But, then, this idea of *yours*, Len – the book you and Lucy have been working on. She told me a little about it, showed me some of it. *So* interesting. The rawness, the revelations and concealments possible in letters.'

What the hell was 'Jeb' short for?

'Hail to the epistolary form!' he cried out of his Jebness, 'that unique vehicle for the heartcry.' His voice was rich – somewhere between Spencer Tracy in *Bad Day At Black Rock* and Eleanor Roosevelt on radio archive records. 'Well, I trust we can talk about what you mean to do with *In Times Of Broken Light* when finished,' he said. 'This would be a great double – to secure for publication, first Lucy, then you. I know your previous fiction, of course, Len – *Placards On High*, *Nursery Scimitar*. Their startling, and yet at the same time utterly natural and integrated symbolism – the snail farm and Ivor's virtual obsession with umbrellas. Lucy has lent me her copies now. I have them in the rucksack. I *must* reread. I could never understand why these books didn't appear in the States. Well, perhaps this could be remedied now – on the back of *In Times Of Broken Light*. Since September eleventh oh-one, I've noticed a new thirst for symbolism in American readers. All publishers have. Perhaps the real – what you would call the nitty-gritty – has become too much to take and hence taste for the oblique, even the mystical.'

Maldave thought of that *Warballs* column in the satirical magazine, *Private Eye*, which collected and quoted crazy, laboured references to the effects of the twin towers catastrophe. Jeb obviously knew about putting on a show. Hadn't he tried with his claim to have read *Placards On High* and *Nursery Scimitar*? Those details he mentioned – the snail farm and Ivor Kemp's comic umbrellas tendency – they certainly existed in the books, but came very near the start of each. Once he heard he was going to meet Maldave, Jeb might have flipped open Lucy's copies of the novels looking for something to quote that might suggest familiarity. A standard social ploy. Len recalled a scene in Trollope's *The Eustace Diamonds* where Lizzie Eustace gets by heart a snippet from the beginning of Shelley's *Queen Mab* for display purposes. And the narrator says that, to pretend she'd read the whole thing, she should have picked verses from the middle or end.

Trollope? *The Eustace Diamonds*? Oh, God, God, Maldave wished, wished, he could ditch this damn pedantry, not feel obliged always to find parallels to life in his reading. And even while he was wishing, wishing this, he thought to himself that the *Queen Mab* episode came a good way into Trollope's novel, which proved Len had really read it right through! Couldn't he feel secure unless able to compare bits of his life with bits in books? Couldn't he exist without print-on-paper endorsements, *old* print-on-paper endorsements?

It half bucked Len up to think of his work on Lucy's shelves, but also half bludgeoned him. How come Jeb was in Lucy's place groping her books and so on? Where was he staying? With her? Damn, she might even have briefed him about *Placards* and *Scimitar* and supplied the references. Did that mean *she* had managed only a few pages of each? Couldn't he reach her at all – through his writing, or as man to woman? In fact, he wanted the two to be the same. Ideally, there should be perfect overlap. There *was* perfect overlap, dismayingly perfect: it amounted to nothing, twice. He felt some anger with Lucy. He felt left behind by Lucy.

And yet, Maldave also wanted to be warm and kindly to her. As far as he knew he had never slept with any woman whose work the *TLS* gave an acre spread to. Oh, why be so damn cagey? Categorically, he had never slept with any woman whose work the *TLS* gave an acre spread to. He had not slept with all that many women, anyway. It was mad to imagine that, of these, one who'd had big publication in the *TLS* would have failed to mention it when in bed with Len, either before or more probably post, knowing him to be a Creative Writing tutor, author and poet. And Len would hardly be in bed with a woman who did *not* know this. Some pre-sex meetings and conversation were almost sure to have taken place on basic topics, such as where he worked. He thought of himself as a non-one-night-stand person, regrettably accurate because he'd never had the chance of a one-night-stand.

Jeb said: 'The prose and general structure of *In Times Of Broken Light* gets a double vision on the world, the large scale and yet the miniature, the microcosm, too. This is the broad setting and the close-up. Ingenious. Illuminating.' Jeb sang a line quietly, warmly: 'You in your small corner and I in mine,' then said, 'these corners, *so* valid, and yet telling us, also, about universals.'

Maldave thought of some mission hall with harmonizing kids in the US Bible Belt, the type of terrain that put George W. Bush back in. Perhaps the name Jeb come from such a background. Didn't the Old Testament have Jebusites, who might easily get shortened to Jeb? As far as Len could recall, they were usually the enemy. Excellent. He would have liked to be sure Jeb stayed in his small corner and Lucy in hers. Who'd bet on that, though? These two had fixed up damn quick rapport. More than that? Len did not want to think of them *together* in a small corner.

Lucy said: 'What I've done with *In Times Of Broken Light*, Len, is to leave untouched that central, appallingly painful, fragile and dangerous relationship between Jill and Dennis, but to give their romantic attachments outside more thorough detail and passion. You attempted it by hint, of course. Subtlety. Understatement. In its way, magnificent. My feeling was that, although skilled, this might not be enough for readers. And perhaps the publishers you sent the script to sensed that, also.'

Maldave still wondered whether in these additions of explicit passion Lucy wanted to say something to him – to him, not to readers or publishers: a sweet, concealed come-on.

'I leave things undecided at the end,' Lucy said.

'The modern reader does not demand closure, or not in quality fiction, anyway,' Jeb stated. No, he didn't just state it, he *pronounced*, by God. 'I'd even argue that the modern reader of non-genre fiction actually *suspects* closure, despises it as falsification,' Jeb went on. 'The idea of a continuation – so vital, so satisfying. Well, I don't have to prove that with you, Len. We think of how *Placards On High* and *Nursery Scimitar* end, or so to speak end, but invite, or rather *demand*, a sense of full, over-the-horizon futures for the characters. Their lives cannot be confined.'

He'd really got through both? Len had an idea that, grown desperate with London publishers, he might at one stage have sent the original script of *In Times Of Broken Light* to Ingleby and Quarl, New York. He must check his rejections portfolio when he had an hour or two. He tried to recall whether Vanessa or Huw Gance actually read out a bang in the teeth from Ingleby and Quarl during that de-self-iconizing workshop. Of course, the script would probably never have reached anyone as high as Jeb in the company. Some nobody killed it on the slush pile. 'Return to sender.' Ingleby and Quarl rated as high calibre publishers, although not massive, as he'd said. Maldave ought to be thankful that Lucy had got Jeb interested.

And he *would* have been thankful if he didn't think Jeb was interested in Lucy, too, and not just her poetry. Might Jeb pretend enthusiasm for Maldave's work only because Lucy had involved herself in some of it, and Jeb wanted to please her? Maldave loathed the notion that his own prospects could depend on how far Jeb got with Lucy, as her publisher – and so on. Didn't that make him, Maldave, seem insignificant? He already had long sessions of feeling insignificant, anyway. These came more or less self-induced, though. He couldn't take such treatment from Mr Fucking Pea-Jacket. Or perhaps he *had* to take it. Mr *Fucking* Pea-Jacket?

Lucy began to read aloud a few of her additions to *In Times Of Broken Light*. The confidence of tone amazed and even affronted Len for a few minutes: after all, this was somebody intruding upon, shaking up, juggling with, somebody's else's work. An infringement. But soon Maldave found he could forgive her. Yes, Lucy provided mostly sexual episodes, but sex written about with such delicacy and precision that Maldave felt his novel truly transformed by them: transformed from what had been a consistently thumbs-down portrait of relationships to writing much less glib and clichéd in its despair, yet not sentimentalized, not wilfully positive. These relationships leaped off the page somehow, were nothing like the kind of sex-therapist's case histories that Maldave had written, as he now realized. She applied some poetry, because she had some, and to spare. If – if, if – *if* a message existed for him in the joyful beat of her sentences, he longed to spot it and, of course, to respond. He felt awed by what he heard, and yet invited. But – also, of course – Jeb sat there and might be mopping up the same message, as if directed at him, the rucksacking, pea-jacketed, boardroom bastard.

At the end, Jeb gasped and brought his hands together gently three times in front of his face as delighted applause. He said: 'Oh, boy! What I like about that – the end, I mean – what gets to me is, OK, yes, at a first view we have a conventional turn-around-shock short-story end, the kind of thing magazines and Saki specialized in many decades ago. Suddenly, it's not our major characters but someone virtually off-stage. Talk about *ex machina*! And yet it's not overly neat, doesn't reek of sharp technique and the facile. In some ways, I'd say it was open-ended. No curtain. That wonderful perpetuation of the linear we spoke of. The, as it were, conclusive defeat of closure.'

Maldave had to close it then, though. It was three forty-five p.m. They left and he hurried to his class. They seemed prepared to walk now. She must have called the taxi to bring them here because time was short. But why short? Couldn't she have come another day – tomorrow, say – when Len's timetable wouldn't have pressed? Did she and Jeb have plans? He disliked thinking of them in a cab together – he recalled a send-up song: *I'll be Don Ameche in a taxi, honey* – but he also loathed seeing them walk together, that damn rucksack suggesting they were on some grand expedition: conjoint.

As Len drove, something in him wondered whether these two, Lucy and Jeb, had likewise written this last clutch of ripe coitus letters for his novel – or what used to be *his* novel – conjoint and as a pair. Fiction did sometimes keep good pace with the real. Jeb's adulation of 'her' work in *In Times of Broken Light* could be acted and, of course, his repeated spasms of apparent surprise. A scenario. As a publisher he might know, or might think he knew, what kind of tale sold, so perhaps he guided Lucy that way. After all, Lucy's bag was poetry, not prose story telling. They could not let on that he'd been the main contributor, of course. Lucy would realize that, although Maldave might take help from *her*, he'd object to yet another hand stirring what had once been Len's exclusive brew, especially if he thought the hand had also been stirring Lucy. And, if that hand *had* also been stirring Lucy, she would probably expect Len to sense it.

At four o'clock, Maldave had an hour-long Creative Writing workshop class with Vanessa, Gance and the others. Maldave detected at once an exceptional atmosphere, a little like those moments leading to their shot-at-dawn mime the other day. First, they discussed a poem by Daisy Nelmes, but Maldave felt this to be just a token before things reached what mattered. Even so, Maldave found the poem troubling. It seemed to deal with savagely contemptuous attempts by friends and enemies to stop a hack writer from writing. Was it a disguised attack? If so, on whom? Did it get at anyone specific, or simply offer a comment on bad writing? Whose fucking bad writing, though? He felt as he often felt with this lot – lampooned, shredded, targeted.

Daisy turned up at classes more frequently

these days. Good? To Maldave her choice of topic seemed chilly and dangerous for these surroundings. She read it out with good attack, her voice not far off a growl. Oh, God, yes, where did the poem point? Someone called Jack appeared in it. Who he? Might Jack be all of them, herself included? Did she mean Creative Writing and its students and teachers could turn out only crap? Sometimes Len hated how the border between life and what got written down in imitation of life became unclear. Daisy called the piece 'Non-poem'. Well, she would; but an improvement on Non-attendance. The lines figured 'writer's block' – that drying up of inspiration and impulse which could affect anyone. Normally, this affliction rated sympathy. But all of *this* poet's friends/enemies felt delighted by the lovely paralysis silencing him/her because her/his work, when it did get produced, was such shit.

'Your writer's block is such a boon –
for us. This tasteful silence brings
a balm; lets everyone forget
the dumbo drool you publish, Jack.
Instead, take up some dicey role –
Sicilian anti-Mafia judge?

We'd rollickingly mourn. Or maybe
fill your processor with shopping lists,
plus begging letters to a soft-touch aunt...'

they said. And so, these smartarse lines
get hatched from failure to create:
one's always keen to squeeze the most
from what one somehow has – or lacks.
The Author's dead we know, and, yes,
This Poet's stone-eyed lifeless, too.
Yet from the joyous footfalls of
his coffin party let me then concoct
this four-five metred drumbeat: call it thrift?

Len said: 'Sharp.'

'About how to make a poem about not being able to make a poem?' Vanessa said. 'Yes, thrifty. The economics of verse. Sicily's interesting. Isn't Palermo a rival for the City Of Culture award? Are you getting at that, Daisy?'

'No. I didn't think of it.'

'A writer can say more than he/she is aware of,' Maldave intoned, keen to shelter behind a bit of ancient formula.

'Jumbled?' Gance asked. 'Why "*joyous* footfalls of his coffin party"?'

'They're glad he's dead, of course,' Vanessa said. 'That is, dead in the sense that he's not writing – metaphorically dead and so, dead quiet.'

'It's why they tell him to become a judge instead,' Dave Merry said, 'because Sicilian judges get knocked over by the Mafia. Like a dark joke?'

'But overall, what does it mean, Daisy?' Gance said.

Merry said: 'Lucy always insisted you should not ask a poet what he/she meant. All the poet could answer is that what he/she meant is what he/she said in the poem and others could make what they wished of it. The poem *is* what it means.'

Oh, God.

'Might she come back, Dr. Maldave?' Daisy said. 'I mean, now she's famous, Ballaugh and the rest will want her, won't they? Good for the image.'

'And the City Of Culture thing,' Merry said. 'When Liverpool won they had all sorts of local talent to offer, some current and active, not just the memory of the Beatles. Lucy is current and active here. Or *was* here until the trimming a couple of weeks ago.'

'So *are* you shagging her, Len?' Vanessa asked.

'Lucy and I are on a project together,' Maldave replied.

'Oh,' Vanessa said. 'I'm right then, am I?'

'A project,' Maldave said.

'And will she come back?' Daisy asked. 'There are rumours in our Common Room.'

'Common rumours,' Vanessa remarked.

'I don't know,' Maldave said. And, tragically, he didn't. Nothing about that was discussed at the recent Lucy-Maldave-Jeb meeting in Len's flat. There'd been the reading; there'd been conversation about publishing arrangements for Lucy's poetry collection and *In Times Of Broken Light*, possibly followed by *Placards On High* and *Nursery Scimitar*. Maldave had tried to make her discuss job intentions, but she did not bite.

Vanessa said: 'Please don't get huffy at what I'm going to touch on now, will you, Len?'

'Huffy? About what?' Maldave replied. He could tell the real business of this workshop was imminent.

'As to projects,' Vanessa said.

Maldave said: 'Lucy and I—'

'All right, there's you and Lucy and *your* project. But *we've* hatched a little project, too.'

'We felt you needed more protection, Len, given the job perils here,' Huw Gance said.

'More than what?'

'More than you have at present,' Vanessa said.

'Remember that tale you wrote for *College Collage*, Len?' Gance said. 'About Osmond Vale, the tutor who inadvertently sends in some of his own work on the reverse side of a student's effort, and it's the student's exercise that bowls the publisher over?'

'You mean "See Overleaf",' Maldave said. 'A flimsy *jeux d'esprit*. A mild attempt at surrealism.'

'It gave us an idea, Len,' Gance said. 'We got together to write something and sent it to the *New Yorker*.'

'Well, great,' Maldave said. He did not like the way things were going. 'It's always good to hear one piece of work can prompt another. Think of Fielding's *Tom Jones*, parodying Richardson's *Clarissa* and probably as great as the original.' Plonk, plonk.

'We sent it in your name, Len,' Vanessa replied.

Gance said: 'We thought that if you could say to the Vice-Chancellor you'd just sold a story to the *New Yorker* – I mean, Len, nobody can do much better than the *New Yorker* – if you could say this, your position would be stronger here. That's on top of your novels, obviously. Extra, conclusive cachet.'

Maldave said: 'But this—'

'We heard today the *New Yorker* want it,'

272

Gance replied. 'We used my digs address.'

'You've sold to the *New Yorker*?' Maldave said. He tried to keep the gasp out of his voice, but he gasped. The bloody *New Yorker*! That was a dollar a word and a shop window unequalled in the universe. John Updike published in the *New Yorker*. And Woody Allen. Carver, Capote and Thurber used to. It had a stupendous tradition of finding new talent. Len frequently offered stuff there. Absolutely no go. That was another, separate sheaf of rejections. Thank heaven he'd never circulated those. Apparently, they came in three forms from the *New Yorker*, though Len had experience only of one. He knew about the three because there'd been an evening talk in the department by a visiting editor of the magazine, who spoke of different refusal grades. If your piece was deemed crap you got a printed slip saying sweetly that although someone there had read it 'with interest' they'd pass. For those who came closer to acceptance, the same printed slip arrived, plus a handwritten note beneath the type regretting that they couldn't use this submission but would like to see more. And then, writers who had almost got the nod, yet still not quite – these would cop an actual and personal letter, no printed slip at all, the message, 'Sorry', yet explaining in careful detail why, so the writer could work on it and re-send, or keep in mind the guidance for the next try.

Len had never got beyond the terse printed hand-off. As for a letter of acceptance, or a *New Yorker* cheque, he had no clue what they might look like, but did think he could visualize the cheque's nicely massed money zeros on a tasteful pale green or blue background. Tastefulness he took to be prime at the *New Yorker*, a dandy with a monocle its logo. He would, of course, have let them publish him for *all* zeros – nothing.

'This was a bit of talent from all of us,' Daisy said.

'Do you know what we felt, Len?' Vanessa said. 'We felt this tale, "See Overleaf", to be something of a *cri de coeur* by you. It exposed a fear that you might be slipping – the older, established talent threatened by youngsters coming up. That's so fucking sad. And, of course, so unwarranted.'

Maldave said: 'Oh, I—'

'He's dead at the end of the tale, isn't he as I recall it – Vale the tutor,' Gance said. 'Death's dark vale, or Vale. Same as the Jack in Daisy's poem, maybe. Well, we decided it shouldn't be like that for you, Len. So we transformed the basic thought. We sort of resurrected you – did some kiss-of-life.'

It was insulting, it was insolent, it was charity, it was a brilliant upending of the theme of 'See Overleaf', it was a magnificent, emotionally overwhelming gift. They claimed the whole class had composed their tale, whatever it might be. But Maldave thought only Gance would have the cheek and cleverness and unexpected warmth to create the overall idea. Perhaps the others had chipped in a word or phrase or two, but the concept and drive must be Huw Gance's.

'You'll be stronger, Dr. Maldave,' Daisy said. 'This was our only object.'

'You'll be able to argue with Ballaugh better for the return of Lucy if he asks your advice – and he might now, you being on the City Of Culture Committee,' Vanessa said.

Maldave's head felt clouded. The *New Yorker* triumph, in a sense, amounted to a community triumph, a triumph of the class combined: the kind of gospel behind Outreach. But the aim of submitting the article seemed to contradict that. Len had to argue with Ballaugh, and those controlling Ballaugh from Westminster, for the reinstatement of a unique, élite, glistening talent: Lucy Corth. In any case, Maldave believed the *New Yorker* tale had, in fact, been instigated and directed by the only real talent in the class, and sometimes a fucking infuriating talent, Gance. Yes, Maldave would, of course, never say so, but, when he placed the irritating undergraduate Robin Maze in 'See Overleaf', he had almost certainly been thinking of Gance. The tale contained in disguised form the worst horror Maldave could visualize: the paper humiliation of Osmond Vale (Maldave) by Robin Maze (Gance). Was something like it happening now? Lately, it had startled Maldave to find his name anagramized into Mad Vale, never mind about death's dark vale, Vale. A writer never knew how much he might give away of her/himself.

'You're not offended are you, Len?' Vanessa asked. 'It's not meant to be patronizing. I'm sure if you wrote something yourself the *New Yorker* would jump at it.'

'I *have* thought now and then of sending them a contribution when I've got time to knock a piece together,' Maldave replied.

'We were only sort of anticipating that Len,' Gance said. 'Like Plato?'

'Plato?' Maldave said.

'He preaches the perfection of the idea, just the idea. The working out of it is secondary, artisan. We knew you'd have the perfect idea. We merely put it into a form, Len. We had to speed things up so you'd be more influential as a Lucy advocate.'

And when Maldave was called to see Ballaugh after the class, he saw the students had been really thorough in their preparations. Somehow, Ballaugh knew about the *New Yorker* acceptance and seemed ready to treat Maldave as valuable, formidable, undeniably talented. Just before Len went into his four p.m. class, Coral, their Departmental Secretary, said the Vice-Chancellor had phoned and would like to see him immediately after his teaching. 'About what?' he asked. Coral, a lean bruiser, very close to her golfing, lay preaching and archery retirement, knew or intuited more or less everything that went on, or was due to go on, in the university.

'Oh, do be sensible, Len, it will be about Lucy Corth, won't it?' she said.

'Will it?'

'You're, well … in exceptional touch with her, aren't you? That's not meaning anything untoward, but, in exceptional touch with her, aren't you?'

'She's a colleague.'

'Was.'

'Well, yes, was,' he said.

'Untenured. Patently.'

'Still a colleague.'

'Such as after the *College Collage* thing –

didn't you give her big attention, at least words of consolation?'

'I helped her get calm again.'

'Brandy, I understand,' Coral said.

'This can have a sedative effect.'

'And then leaving the campus together?'

'We had some work to discuss.'

'Work? She doesn't work here any more.'

'Private work.'

'Where?'

'What?'

'This discussion,' she replied. 'Your place? Her place?'

'You're right. It didn't really matter where,' Maldave replied. 'The only aim was to get her away from the scene. Imperative, as I judged it. Change of location – a sort of therapy.'

'That right? Do you want my guess?'

'As to what?' Maldave asked.

'Why Ballaugh wants to see you.'

'Why?'

'This university's made a total muck up, hasn't it? The Government likewise. Sacked a genius.'

'Lucy Corth's had a success, yes,' he replied.

'I'm told "unprecedented". That's the term I keep getting, and from people who know. Sam Oballe for one.'

'Certainly unusual.'

'They want you to whistle her back, Len, because you're obviously a deep pal, filling her with brandy, taking her home.'

'Whistle her back?'

'Persuade her to forget she was fired. Persuade her to forgive. They think she'll listen to you.'

'Who do?'

'The V-C. And most likely Elton Dape, in charge of the touting campaign for City Of Culture, if he's heard you managed to liquor her up, then slipped off with her to give her – what did you call it, "calm". This is an exceptional looking girl.'

'Not slipped off. Accompanied her.'

'Slipped off is how it will look to Dape. He does his share of slipping off with girls himself, doesn't he? You're on the Committee. You must have heard that. He'll think and hope you have a ... well, an *entrée* to Corth.'

How the information about the *New Yorker* had reached Ballaugh, Maldave couldn't tell, but it would be Gance. Perhaps a word to Oballe, head of English, who would then pass it on. 'I've tried in my own rather foolish way to approach Corth,' Ballaugh said now at their meeting in his suite, 'but have decided I must call on you, Leonard. She will respect you and your achievements, including the latest, for which, congratulations. You can offer her full staff status, and bugger the budget.'

'I don't think Lucy will do it without A. F. W. Ichbald.'

'A. F. W. as fucking well,' Ballaugh replied. 'That's the price. My fear is Lucy might go to Wales.'

'Oh?'

'Eider.'

'What's that?'

'A V-C. A sort of friend. And enemy. He'd take her, the scheming lout.'

'Her CV must be very glossy now.'

'Her CV's part of it, yes. Part of it. They'll snare her. She'll be gone. Can you want that?' Ballaugh said.

No, he couldn't want that. But, then, he couldn't want Jeb around her either, though he was, wasn't he?

And when Maldave's bell rang at home next day, he assumed Lucy and Jeb had come back for further talks about *In Times Of Broken Light*. That did not please Maldave a hundred per cent. He felt glad the book might – well, *would* – get published in America and then, most probably, picked up by a British firm, but he wanted to talk privately, very privately, to Lucy about the new material she'd provided, and see where things went from there. He noticed no face-wide grin in the hall mirror as he went to open the door this time.

Lucy stood there alone.

'Where's Jeb?' he said.

'He's gone to his hotel,' she replied.

'He's staying in a hotel?'

'Well, of course. Where else?' She gave Len a short stare. 'Oh, I see. You thought—'

They went into the sitting room. 'I've got some gin,' he said and found the bottle and some tonic.

She said: 'Quarl returns to the States tomorrow. We can send him the script when you've checked everything and polished it. He insists we do.'

He delighted in this – the surname only for Jeb, the 'we' for her and Len. And a pretty fatuous surname, Quarl, though he wouldn't mind it too much as publishing house, or half the publishing house, on the spine bottom of an *In Times Of Broken Light*'s dust jacket. 'Send him the novel? I'll drink to that,' he replied, drinking to that.

She had the chair Quarl sat in yesterday. She suited it better. He resented the implied arse contact via an unchanged cushion though. 'Ballaugh, tailing like that yesterday – he really wants me at the department again?'

'You didn't see him following this time?'

'Not today. I went out the back way and jumped on a bus.'

'Yes, he really wants you reinstated.'

'You know this? How?'

He'd been reluctant to say Ballaugh asked him to middleman. He didn't want to come over to her as a messenger boy. But now he did tell her about the meeting and the offer.

'He'll forgive me?' she said

'Forgive you? Sorry, I don't see that. What about putting it as, Will you forgive *him*, and the Minister and Ministers?'

'You *do* remember my little confrontation with Ballaugh, though, after the sacking? Is it *really* forgivable?'

'In *Trainspotting* "cunt" is almost an endearment,' Maldave replied.

'Oh, I didn't mean it like that, not at the time, no endearment. Not as far as Ballaugh was concerned. He stood back and let A. F. W. and me suffer for the sake of … of a damn fees campaign.' Lucy nodded reflectively two or three times. 'Apart from its use to label him, yes, I suppose the C-word *should* be an endearment.'

Odd to hear her bowdlerize it, after the *College Collage* hearty frankness. 'I often think this,' Len replied.

'Do you? How often?'

'A. P. Herbert, or someone like, wrote a verse saying, strange that such an ugly word should refer to such a—'

'*Can* words be ugly?' she replied. 'In themselves?'

'Some words can surely be beautiful, can't they? And so the reverse should be true.'

'Which words can be beautiful?'

'"Azure." "Lacustrine."'

'Beautiful apart from their meaning?'

'Ah.'

'Can some seemingly ugly words, like the C-word, become beautiful, sort of redeemed, when associated with what they signify?' she asked.

He thought this conversation good and incisive and forward-looking. At least, *he* was looking forward. It provided a move on from the kind of oblique, clouded messages he might have looked for in her *In Times Of Broken Light* letters. This talk went direct to what could be regarded as the centre. 'I'm really glad you came back here and alone, Lucy,' he said.

'Quarl wanted to as well. I decided it would be better not. I don't think he saw the situation properly – its intricacies.'

'No.'

The intricacies began sweetly to take over then and in his bed later he said: 'The

283

students miss you.' He was thinking of the class's *New Yorker* ploy and that moment when someone quoted Lucy's rule about not interrogating the poet. 'We had a terribly negative piece of work yesterday called "Non-poem", and I sensed that it came from this whole damn awful situation – questioning the entire validity of C. W. They're confused, demoralized. It's caught up on them. They can still be clever, yes, but clever-cynical.'

'And *I* miss *them*,' she replied. She had held his head, one hand on each temple, as they made love, as if she wanted to keep his face still while she watched it, recording his delight and fulfilment. He thought if anyone ought to be looking at a face it was he at hers, but he knew he might not be able to manage this, not without the delight and fulfilment galloping through him too damn fast, so he kept his eyes shut. He felt very aware, though of those kindly hands just above his ears, like an infinitely comfortable balaclava.

'So, you'll come back?' he said, eventually. 'We've still got a lot to do on *In Times Of Broken Light* before we send it to Jeb.'

'That's the only reason you want me to stay?'

'Naturally,' he replied. She was lying on

top of him, spreadeagled, a bit exhausted. 'Oh, yes, naturally.'

She stirred slightly and he stirred slightly, also, but might do better in a few minutes. 'I don't believe you,' she said.

'No. Good. We're expert in irony, you know, C. W. folk. It's nearly non-stop.'

'But I wouldn't go back without A. F. W.'

'A. F. W. is included.'

'Sure?'

'Sure.'

Next morning they visited together A. F. W.'s flat, in the Old Canal district of the city, to check the offer was acceptable. Decent, distorted pride might obstruct. 'Dave Merry and I were shacked up, you know,' A. F. W. said. 'I'd begun to get him off coke, or at least persuade him to use both nostrils. But the strain of all this – we split.'

'Yes, I feared that,' Maldave said.

'It was really tough, sad,' Lucy said.

'If you come back it might all turn right again,' Maldave said.

'Well, it might, yes,' A. F. W. replied.

Twelve

Ballaugh heard from Len Maldave that Lucy would return, Lucy *and* A. F. W. Ichbald. From his suite at the university, Ballaugh at once telephoned Basil Roffe, head of the Creative Writing Department and asked if he could pop over and see him. He tried to keep his voice light and the words informal, not darkened by Dape-type Power, but he thought Bas would guess what it was about. Roffe must have seen Lucy in the *TLS* and had probably heard something of student discontent over the loss of her. Basil might even have grapevined he had been out lunching with Dape, and suspect he and the city wanted Corth re-engaged soonest.

Of course, Basil Roffe had fought to keep Lucy and Ichbald employed. That did not mean, though, that he would now readily agree to have them reinstated. He might think decisions should be stuck to, even wrong ones. He could be difficult. Perhaps he'd feel shilly-shallying was bad for the department's reputation and bad for the university's, too. He would probably see a political plot in the moves over Corth and Ichbald. He'd be right. He might not like the idea that Ballaugh could exercise more or less autocratic power – today people fired, tomorrow invited back – all on his dictatorial say-so. Ballaugh had not, after all, flouted university employment rules by sacking Corth and Ichbald and the rest. The wording in probationary contracts was strongly explicit about absence of tenure. In a way, these two had had the kind of agreement that Gabriel occupied now while waiting for his fully confirmed dog wardenship. No guarantees existed. That's why Elton Dape and his Power mattered so much.

'Outreach, Vice-Chancellor,' Basil said almost as soon as he arrived. Roffe had always seemed part doubtful about the concept but seemed enthusiastic now.

'Well, yes,' Ballaugh replied.

'Something's come up.'

'Yes?'

'I'm glad you asked me to see you,' Basil said.

'It's a matter—'

'This could be called an outcrop of Outreach,' Basil replied, and giggled. He seemed nervous, but not in the manner Ballaugh had been expecting. Bas wore a burgundy leather bomber jacket and jeans. He had a square, rather blank, fattish face which today, though, seemed very chirpy and challenging. Ballaugh did not much like this. His script required one of two kinds of attitude from Bas: a kind of stubborn, pedantic defiance of the *status quo*, despite his previous championing of Corth and Ichbald; or a crowing acceptance of their return – a chance to prove he had been correct all along. His appearance and behaviour now did not seem to match either of these reactions, though. He bubbled with – with what? Joy? Fun? Anticipation? So, *what* fucking outcrop from fucking Outreach? Don't bring your damn C. W. wordplay here.

'Yes, as you know, Vice-Chancellor, I've had reservations over Outreach but now I feel it should extend and extend,' Basil said, 'be a developing, living process. It was the half-cock, tentative application of Outreach that may have put me off a little before.'

'Right.' Some claptrap must always be allowed in any discussions on educational policy.

'I wanted to go further than the "Poems and Pints" thing – sessions in pubs. That might have once been new and bold, but now rates only as workaday and corny.'

'The Minister was impressed with accounts he'd heard of our Outreach. Very much what he hoped for.'

'Oh, the Minister. What does he know about anything?'

'Well, he—'

'What he was looking for was pussy.'

'The Minister has a specific notion of what he wants from C. W. Departments.'

'Pussy. You had him at your house, I heard. Your wife there? But I expect she'd know how to keep that sort off.'

'Look, Basil, what I really—'

'OK, poets and pints fine. As an extension to that, though, I wanted to try something with a younger, perhaps brasher, more fun-orientated clientèle.'

That word, 'fun'. The flavour of it seemed to possess Basil today. Eerie. Belated.

'Yes, the fun element in writing – so crucial,' Roffe said. 'It can't all be elegy style. So I thought, a disco.'

'That's damn enterprising.' Outreach really had come to outreach for Bas.

'It's tricky,' he said.

'Yes, strobe lighting. Dodgy for readings,' Ballaugh replied.

'Not many intervals. Kids want non-stop-ness.'

'Right. My son Piers often mentioned the

importance of disco non-stopness.'

'But if I could get something into one of these pauses which really reached the dancers – reached! – you see? – reached, *Outreached* – then they'd want more. One must believe in the product wholeheartedly if it's to take off.'

'Right. Could you?'

'What?'

'Reach them,' Ballaugh said. Should he be listening to all this? He had called Bas here to discuss Lucy Corth, for him to be told clearly, though not necessarily bluntly, about Lucy Corth redux.

'Vice-Chancellor, I've had a trial and it worked. Short readings. One-scene drama. Mime.'

'Ichbald was into mime, I gather.'

'There are others. Upshot, anyway, is we have a regular disco venue for Outreach.'

'Which?'

'Optimum.'

'Ah, Amy Burdage-Pask's place? She's very pro-student, isn't she? Always takes advertising space in *College Collage*. Did I see her chatting with you at the ... at the party?' In fact, Burdage-Pask's face was one of the clearest recollections Ballaugh had of that birthday celebration for the magazine. He remembered noting her in apparently consoling conversation with Bas after the Lucy outburst, but also, before that, gazing delightedly at Lucy, tall on her chair, as if she thought this some kind of brilliant, planned, entertainment event.

'I could never have got this new venue for Outreach going without her help and enthusiasm,' Roffe said.

Ballaugh believed he suddenly caught a warming, a tremor, in not just Roffe's voice but his whole physique when he spoke of Burdage-Pask. It seemed beyond what might come from gratitude for the Optimum Outreach. Bas gave one of those smiles where there seemed more teeth than was right for any human mouth, each bright with message. Ballaugh said: 'Basil, what I really wanted to talk about—'

'Lucy Corth.'

'And A. F. W. Ichbald.'

'Corth, mainly, isn't it?' Roffe replied. They were in armchairs on the polished board floor space to the side of his desk. The secretary had brought in coffee.

Roffe watched him, but without aggression or contempt, Ballaugh thought, and possibly in a do-a-deal fashion. What deal? 'I don't in any way question your right to run C. W. as seems proper to you,' Ballaugh said.

'You want Corth re-employed despite

everything?'

'And Ichbald, suppose they agree.'

'Ichbald's a nobody. A makeweight in the case. It's entirely about Corth, isn't it?'

'I can't think of members of university staff as nobodies,' Ballaugh intoned.

'Ichbald is *not* a member of university staff.'

'No, well—'

Basil said: 'You'll have heard about my wife.'

'No. No, I don't think I have.'

'Well, perhaps it figures you haven't heard of her She's not around all that often.'

Ballaugh found it tough trying to keep pace. Would things come back to Corth eventually? And how long was eventually?

'Simone's a cartographer, you know. Mapping,' he said. 'Oh, sorry. Of course you'll know the word. The deal was, when I landed this job, that she'd take an admin post in London, working two days up there and the rest from home. She's quite senior and could pretty well nominate her own work programme. What she's actually nominated is to do inland New Guinea. She likes apartness.'

Ballaugh thought he glimpsed a theme. 'You've found Amy Burdage-Pask ... well, very understanding?'

'She likes my work.'

'That's important.'

'My verse plays and lighter stuff. She's genuinely interested.'

'I'm sure she would be,' Ballaugh said.

'Do *you* know my writing?'

'*College Collage*,' Ballaugh said. 'Unusual.'

'I can't say my wife ever showed any—'

'Maps can take a hold on people,' Ballaugh replied.

'And, naturally, Amy responds to others' C. W. offerings, not just mine. She's ... she's in touch.'

'Yes.' Ballaugh thought of calling the secretary for replacement coffees, to keep him alert, awake. Jesus, Dape at lunch yesterday, now this lot. But renewed coffee might suggest to Basil they were settling to an even more considerable chat and Ballaugh didn't want to risk that.

Bas twitched in his chair. Ballaugh thought the message might truly be near. Roffe said: 'The thing is, Vice-Chancellor, Amy Burdage-Pask has become very keen – keen and constructive – on the European City Of Culture concept.'

'Ah.'

'Optimum is an innovative idea, you know, as discos go. It's not at all run-of-the-mill in ambience and purpose.'

'If it has taken Outreach aboard it *must* be

distinctive.'

'Even without that,' he said. 'Amy has given it a ... a uniqueness. I don't think this is to overstate.'

'An achievement.'

'Amy would greatly like the city bid to succeed, and to be a part of the portfolio. She feels, and I share the view, that Optimum would justly take on a European status as a centre for the presentation of current music. The way Ronnie Scott's is for jazz in London, or some of those clubs in Copenhagen and Barcelona. Cachet. Optimum already has cachet. But to internationalize.'

'This is a great ambition.'

Roffe nodded, then shrugged – a so-what movement now. 'You're no doubt thinking I've amended my attitude rather towards the ECOC campaign. You'll remind me I would not sit on the Committee but sent Len Maldave. Well, I've gone rather rapidly from hostility, via indifference, to enthusiasm, as I suppose I have about Outreach.'

Yes, and Ballaugh thought he saw why. 'We all change our minds.' He recalled Fiona talking of Basil's possible need for community support, perhaps comradely support, if his wife were eternally away doing her maps. Perhaps he had found some good and continuing comradeship from Burdage-Pask, who was sympathetic to his work and, crucially, much closer than New Guinea. 'You'll want the city's application to be strong, then,' he replied.

'Now, as to Corth,' Roffe replied.

'She would be an asset in the campaign.'

'I'm not going to make a rumpus if you bring her back. I can see the reasoning.'

'And Ichbald.'

'Ichbald's a nothing.'

'It's vital for equity,' Ballaugh said.

'Oh, I appreciate that. Of course, the city could tout Lucy as a local, whether or not she's re-employed here. But it's probably a better point if she's not just local but part of the local university. Yes.'

Ballaugh identified the deal now. Roffe would not object in his customary, pedantic way to the *volte face* on Lucy if Amy Burdage-Pask could be supported by Ballaugh as part of the city's competitive Culture items.

'Perhaps I'll alternate with Len at the Literature Committee,' Roffe said. 'I hear local historian Stanley Ivens is working on a theory that Henry Fielding might have come looking for a gout cure to a quack in this area. Fascinating. I mean to get myself known to the organizers of the ECOC bid in general.'

Also he'd get dear Amy Burdage-Pask known. 'I think Maldave will successfully bring Lucy back – and Ichbald,' Ballaugh said.

'It's finalized, is it?' Roffe replied.

Only a few moments after he left, Mo came on the phone again from Westminster. 'A sort of farewell, Casp,' he said.

'Farewell?'

'I'm moving from Education. A reshuffle next week – confidential for the moment, but I naturally felt a duty to ring certain friends in advance.'

'Thanks, Mo.'

'Defence.'

'What?'

'I go to Defence. It's a leg-up.'

'Do you know anything about Defence?' Ballaugh said.

'It's been very fruitful, Casp.'

'What?'

'Working with you, meeting Fiona.'

'Basil says she'd be used to keeping people like you from groping her and so on,' Ballaugh said.

'The point about Ministerial changes is that someone coming from, say, Education to Defence, brings an utterly fresh brain, uninhibited by previous Defence thinking,' Mo replied. 'No actual *knowledge* but clearheadedness, drive. The Civil Servants *know* things. That's *their* function. We are for the people and provide the overview with that basic axiom in mind.'

'Which?'

'For the people.'

'We've got Lucy Corth back,' Ballaugh replied.

'Corth? Lucy?'

'The girl crucial for the City Of Culture campaign.'

'Ah.'

'Not easy.'

'I'm transferring to Iraq, possibly Iran, terrorism, that kind of thing now,' Mo replied. 'Logistics. The whole caboodle. Sand problems for our tanks.'

'Who'll take over this side of things?'

'Ah, yes – Corth, Lucy. I remember now. Great tits, did I hear? You'll be OK there then, Casp, if you've been able to pull her back. Lucky old you, Casp. And I think there was talk of a peerage, wasn't there? I'll leave a definite memo on that to my successor.'

'Who is it, Mo?'

'We're all equally for the people, you know, regardless of which particular Ministry.'

'Being for the people's fine, but as you know the City Of Culture campaign is—'

'And merging regiments,' Mo said. 'Controversial. I'll be involved there. It's what we call in Government "a challenge". But, as you appreciate, I enjoy that, Casp.'

It was a Friday. Ballaugh went to the mirror bar in the evening and sat alone with a Cointreau. He thought the lighting under the glass had been increased as if someone sought to poke deeper into his image and interior. Such scrutiny Ballaugh did not mind. He brought pain and frustration and confusion and required them illuminated. He wanted Hopper interested, or the idea of Hopper, who died decades ago. But Ballaugh had the dismal feeling that Hopper would not, in fact, have painted him. Ballaugh considered he no longer looked like a symbol of many, many tortured lives. He looked ... he looked dismal, just that. The cuff-link platoons from the offices, barristers' chambers, executive suites might be better symbols. Raucous, lively, assured, they didn't need constant mirror therapies. They had something going and meant to keep it going.

After a while, Fiona came in and sat on the stool next to him. He asked whether she'd like a gin and French or advocaat. She asked for rum and black.

He said: 'But in the poem you—'

'I thought you'd be here,' she said. 'You

298

take things so plain and literally, don't you, Casp? It's the Economics training. Did you notice that novel in the bookshop window next door?'

'Which?'

'The title is *I Am Charlotte Simmons*, but the writer is Tom Wolfe. You see? What we read or have read to us is not necessarily how things are. And a poem's just a poem.'

'Is it? Fiona, do you know somewhere near, somewhere we could go?'

'How would I?'

'Like in the poem.'

'It's a poem.'

'Let's find that sort of place, then, shall we? It would mean something to me if we can act it out,' Ballaugh said.

'Shall we?'

'Please. Did Mo try anything?'

'Mo?'

'The Minister.'

'I remember him. Outreach?'

'Did he outreach to you?' Ballaugh said.

'I find I do get a kick from strolling the length of the bar, men watching, but my only object you, Casp, in front of the mirror.'

'That right? Is that really right, Fiona? How did you know about this bar for the poem in the first place, and what it was like to walk through?'

'And now we can walk back out together, a sort of affirmation. A kind of declaration that all these cuff-linked prats can fuck off. We've got continuance, we've got the past, we've got now and what comes next. Two fine sons in the media and official dog wardenship. Oh, yes, Casp, Gabriel rang. He's qualified, ratified, and might get a management course.'

'Dape must really—'

'Who?'

'Dape. He's Culture. And acts. He must really have pressured Ollie, because of Lucy.'

'Who?'

'They say a mirror doesn't show you as you really are, it's all reversed.'

She downed her drink. 'We should move?'

'To the experienced sheets? You definitely weren't expecting someone else here to-night, were you, Fiona? Is that why you're hurrying to get out before he turns up?'

'But in the poem he's early. It's *you* who were early, Casp.'